Lethal Beauty Inside the Minds of Women Who Kill

Morgan B. Blake

Published by CopyPeople.com, 2024.

Table of Contents

"Even the most beautiful roses have thorns."

CopyPeople

The Caretaker's Love

Maggie had always had a soft spot for the elderly. She couldn't explain it; it was as if she could feel their loneliness, their desperation for companionship, even if they could no longer voice it. Growing up, she spent her days visiting nursing homes, volunteering in the afternoons, and sitting with those who were too forgotten by family or too weak to fend for themselves. As a teenager, she had promised herself that one day, she would make sure that the elderly were never left alone in their final years.

By the time Maggie was in her thirties, she had done what she set out to do. She opened her own home care service, calling it *Golden Years Care*. It was small at first, just a few elderly clients scattered across the neighborhood. But soon, as word of mouth spread, her business grew. People trusted her; they trusted her soft, kind smile, the soothing tone of her voice, and the caring way she handled her clients. She was everything they needed: reliable, compassionate, and devoted.

For Maggie, it was more than just a job—it was a calling. She never saw it as work. She saw it as her purpose, her mission to ease the pain and suffering of the old, the infirm, the ones society had long forgotten. She was their angel, their salvation, the only one who could restore dignity to their final years.

It wasn't long before the authorities began noticing something strange. An unusual number of deaths had been reported among her clients in the last six months. The deaths weren't directly linked—heart attacks, strokes, pneumonia. But there was an undeniable pattern: most of them had been under her care at the time of their passing. It was subtle, just a few whispers in the wind at first, but when one of her clients, a woman named Edna, died in the middle of a routine check-up, the whispers turned into calls for investigation.

Detective Reynolds was the one assigned to the case. He was a man of few words, his experience in the field making him both cautious and methodical. He wasn't quick to judge, but the evidence was mounting. Maggie's clients had all passed away quietly, without struggle, and with no signs of foul play—at least, none that would immediately raise alarm. But the sheer number of deaths made it impossible to ignore. Someone, he thought, was covering their tracks.

Reynolds' first meeting with Maggie was in her office, a small, neat room decorated with photographs of smiling families and well-wishers. Maggie greeted him with a smile that seemed to put him at ease immediately. She was a woman in her forties, her hair pulled back in a simple bun, her eyes soft and welcoming.

"Detective Reynolds, what can I do for you?" she asked, offering him a seat.

"I'm investigating the recent deaths of some of your clients," he said, not bothering with small talk. "I know you're busy, but I'll need to ask you a few questions."

Maggie nodded, her smile never faltering. "Of course. Anything you need."

He started with the basics—names, addresses, dates of death. She answered each question without hesitation, her calm demeanor making it difficult for him to believe she could be involved in anything sinister. But something in the back of his mind nagged at him, a growing discomfort that he couldn't shake.

Over the following weeks, Reynolds continued his investigation, tracking Maggie's clients, checking medical records, and speaking with family members. Every piece of the puzzle seemed to fit perfectly: her clients had all been elderly, frail, often with a host of medical issues. Some of them had even expressed how relieved they were to have Maggie by their side, how much peace she brought them in their final days.

But the more he dug, the more he found that couldn't be explained. A pattern emerged. A disturbing pattern.

In each case, Maggie had been the one to administer the final dose of medication—an extra pill, a bit more than prescribed, slipped into a glass of water or hidden in a bowl of soup. It was subtle enough to go unnoticed, enough to make the death look natural. But Reynolds knew it wasn't. The doses weren't accidental. They were deliberate. And Maggie had been the only one with access to the medication.

By the time Reynolds had enough evidence to confront her, Maggie had already anticipated his every move. She had a way of knowing, a way of making you feel like you were the one out of place, the one who didn't belong.

When he confronted her in her office, the air between them was thick with tension. "I know what you're doing, Maggie," he said, his voice hard. "You've been killing your clients."

Maggie didn't flinch. She didn't even look surprised. She simply leaned back in her chair, her hands folded neatly in her lap. "Detective, you're mistaken. I'm only doing what I've always done: helping them."

He narrowed his eyes. "Helping them? By killing them?"

"They were suffering, Detective. They were old, they were in pain. Some of them were ready to go, but they couldn't. They needed someone to help them cross over. And that's what I did."

Reynolds' heart pounded as he stared at her. He didn't know whether to feel disgusted or awed. "You took their lives into your own hands."

"I gave them peace," she corrected, her voice gentle, almost soothing. "I've always given them peace. You don't understand, Detective. They were begging for it. They wanted to die."

It hit him then—the twisted logic of it all. Maggie had convinced herself that she was doing them a favor, that she was giving them the release they couldn't ask for. She wasn't just a murderer. She was a savior in her own mind. And in the minds of her clients, maybe she had been.

But Reynolds wasn't finished. "And what about Edna? The one who didn't want to go?" he asked, his voice steady.

Maggie's smile faltered for just a moment, before she masked it again. "Edna... Edna was special. She didn't ask for my help. She wasn't ready. But she was in so much pain, Detective. I had to... I had to make her understand. I had to help her, too."

Reynolds stared at her, feeling the weight of her words settle into his bones. She didn't feel guilty. She didn't regret it. In her mind, she had done nothing wrong.

"I'm sorry, Maggie," he said softly. "You're going to prison."

But as he stepped out of the office, Maggie watched him go, her smile returning once again.

The lesson was clear. Sometimes, those who believe they are doing the right thing can become blind to the horror they've caused. Maggie had wanted to ease the suffering of others, but in her twisted devotion to that ideal, she had become the very thing she had sworn to fight against: a killer.

The Mercy of Judgment

Samantha had always known she was meant to help people. Growing up, she admired her mother's work as a nurse, the way she could comfort the sick and ease their pain with a gentle touch and a soft word. It was no surprise when Samantha followed in her mother's footsteps, becoming a nurse herself and finding a job in a local cancer ward. The ward was filled with the dying, patients who were often in unbearable pain, suffering from diseases that twisted their bodies and souls. It was a place where death was a constant companion, a waiting room for the inevitable.

At first, Samantha threw herself into her work with the kind of dedication that came naturally to her. She learned the names of every patient, remembered their stories, their families, their loves, and their losses. She was their caretaker, their lifeline, the one who held their hands when the chemotherapy was too much, who wiped their brows when the fever spiked. She was good at it—too good, maybe. She listened to them, comforted them, and did everything she could to make their final days bearable. But slowly, over time, she began to grow tired. The endless suffering, the pain that didn't seem to end, the cries for help that no one could answer—it all weighed on her. The system, the doctors, the treatments—they all seemed so useless in the end.

As she spent more time in the ward, she began to hear whispers—whispers from patients who spoke in the dark of the night, when they thought no one was listening. "I'm ready," they would say, their voices barely above a whisper. "I just want it to stop." They spoke not just of their pain but of their hopelessness, their exhaustion with fighting a battle they knew they could never win. Samantha would listen, nodding, comforting, but inside, a small seed of doubt began to take root.

She saw the doctors give up on patients, telling them there was nothing more they could do. She saw families sit by their loved ones' bedsides, looking weary and defeated, waiting for the inevitable. And then there were the others—the patients who didn't seem to deserve it. The ones who were cruel, who screamed at the nurses, who complained incessantly about their treatment. The ones who seemed to wallow in their misery, unwilling to face the reality of their situation. She began to wonder: What if there was another way to end their suffering?

It was a simple thought at first, a fleeting moment when she considered what it might be like to offer them a little more relief, a little more peace. But the thought kept coming back, creeping into her mind with a kind of urgency that she couldn't ignore. And then, one day, when an especially cruel and selfish patient named Alan, who had been complaining nonstop about his diagnosis and tormenting the staff with his foul attitude, asked her for more painkillers, Samantha didn't hesitate.

She had never been the type to act impulsively, but in that moment, it felt like the right thing to do. Alan was suffering, yes, but more than that, he was exhausting everyone around him. The endless complaints, the cruelty he unleashed on others—it was a constant drain on the emotional resources of the staff and patients. He would never appreciate the life he had left. He would never show gratitude for the care he received. What harm would it do, she thought, to end it a little sooner? Just enough to bring peace to the ward, to herself, to everyone around him.

She injected him with an overdose of pain medication, a dose high enough to kill but low enough to look like a complication of his condition. He died that night, quietly, without struggle, without fanfare. Samantha felt a strange sense of relief as she filled out the death certificate, her hands steady as she recorded the cause of death. No one questioned it. It seemed natural. Alan had been suffering for so long. Perhaps this was just a little extra mercy.

As the weeks went by, the feeling of control began to settle into Samantha's bones. She didn't just provide comfort anymore. She offered what she called "the ultimate relief." One by one, she began selecting the patients she deemed unworthy of life—those who made the ward a darker place, those whose suffering seemed endless, whose bitterness stained the air. She didn't do it for them. She did it for herself, for the peace of the ward, for the lives of the other patients. She was offering them mercy, after all. And if some lives were cut short, wasn't that a small price to pay for the greater good?

But as time wore on, Samantha's actions didn't go unnoticed. It wasn't the doctors or nurses who began to question her, but the patients themselves. Some started to whisper. There were rumors—small things, at first—about how certain patients had died so suddenly, so quietly. How some had seemed to slip away in the middle of the night, when no one was watching. But Samantha was careful. She had learned to cover her tracks, to make every death look natural, to hide the truth behind the veil of kindness.

It wasn't until one of the patients, an elderly woman named Eleanor, began to suspect something, that things started to unravel. Eleanor had been a patient for months, bedridden and unable to move, but still sharp in mind. She had seen too many deaths, too many changes in the ward, and something in her gut told her that not all of them had been natural. She kept an eye on Samantha, watched her every move with suspicion, and eventually confronted her one evening when they were alone.

"You've been doing it, haven't you?" Eleanor asked, her voice raspy but firm. "You've been killing them."

Samantha froze, her blood running cold. For the first time, she realized how far she had gone. She had been offering mercy, she had been playing God, and now someone knew.

Eleanor didn't fear death. She had been ready for it for years. But there was something about the way Samantha had taken control of it, the way she had judged others so ruthlessly, that unsettled her deeply. "You think you have the right to decide who lives and who dies? You're no better than the cancer itself."

Samantha's heart pounded in her chest. For a long moment, neither woman spoke. Eleanor's words hung in the air like a dark cloud, suffocating Samantha, pressing her back into her chair. What had she become? She had wanted to help, wanted to give peace, but somewhere along the way, she had crossed a line. She had judged, condemned, and killed—not out of compassion, but out of something darker.

In the end, Samantha did not deny it. She simply smiled—a small, sad, defeated smile—and walked out of the room. The next morning, Eleanor was dead.

The lesson, for Samantha, was clear. In her attempt to offer mercy, she had become a judge, a jury, and an executioner. And like the patients she had killed, she too would never know peace. She had betrayed the very thing that had driven her to nursing: the belief that every life, no matter how small or broken, had value. And now, as she walked the sterile halls of the cancer ward, she realized she was no different from the suffering souls she had tried to end.

The Babysitter's Silence

Maggie had always been the perfect babysitter. She knew how to smile and reassure the parents that their children would be safe, comfortable, and well-cared for. It had become second nature to her over the years—showing up on time, being kind, offering a little extra help when asked, and making sure that the kids had everything they needed. In the eyes of the parents, she was a dream. Responsible. Caring. Attentive.

She wasn't anything special to the children, though. At least not at first. To them, she was just another face, another adult who entered their world and made them do what they didn't want to do: go to bed, eat their vegetables, pick up their toys. But Maggie didn't mind. She didn't do this job for the children. She didn't do it for the parents either, not really. She did it for herself.

She had grown up with parents who rarely paid attention to her. Her mother was distant, always preoccupied with her own issues, and her father wasn't around much. It wasn't that they were bad people—just absent. And so, Maggie learned how to slip under the radar, to blend into the background of her own life, unnoticed, unnoticed for the things she needed, unnoticed for the things she craved. She wanted more—she wanted attention, power, control. She wanted to be needed, to be the one they couldn't live without.

The children she cared for, the ones whose parents relied on her to be their safe haven, were perfect for her purposes. These children came from broken homes, homes where the parents had no idea what was happening behind their closed doors, where neglect was as common as the air they breathed. They weren't wanted. They weren't loved. Their cries fell on deaf ears, their complaints ignored. They lived in worlds where nobody cared to look too deeply, where nobody asked the questions that mattered.

And Maggie took advantage of that. At first, it was small things. She would comfort the children when they cried, but her comfort had a darker edge. She whispered in their ears about how nobody else cared about them, how they didn't matter to anyone except her. And when they were sad or frightened, she would provide solace in a way that no one else did—by making them depend on her.

But Maggie wasn't satisfied with just comforting them. She wanted more. She wanted their pain to be her pleasure. She wanted them to trust her completely, to be so afraid of her absence that they would follow her every command. She wanted them to fear her as much as they needed her. Maggie began to test the limits of her power, testing how far she could push before they would break.

One night, when a boy named Timmy, just five years old, started to cry because he couldn't find his stuffed bear, Maggie found the perfect opportunity. She told him she would find the bear for him, but only if he promised to do exactly as she said. Timmy, desperate for comfort, agreed. Maggie hid the bear in the closet, far out of reach, and then demanded he recite a list of chores—his homework, his toys, his dishes—all the things he should have been doing. She watched as Timmy, frightened and desperate for her approval, did everything she asked, his small hands shaking as he tried to please her. She didn't care about the chores. She didn't care about the bear. All she cared about was how Timmy had bent to her will, how he had given her control over his life, just for a small moment of comfort.

It wasn't long before other children began to disappear. At first, it was just one or two, and no one suspected Maggie. Children from broken homes, children who no one would notice if they were gone for a few days. Parents assumed the children had simply run off or stayed at a friend's house. After all, children often had their own world—where they didn't always inform their parents of their whereabouts. But when one child went missing, and then another, and then another, a quiet suspicion began to form.

Detective Harris was called in to investigate. He had been a cop for years, seen his fair share of cases, but something about this one felt different. He noticed the pattern right away: all the missing children had been cared for by Maggie at some point. They were all from broken families, all neglected in some way. He didn't want to believe it. He wanted to believe it was just coincidence, that there was some other explanation, but he couldn't ignore the way things lined up. He began to dig deeper into Maggie's past, searching for something, anything, that might explain her involvement.

One night, Harris paid her a visit while she was babysitting for a new family. Maggie greeted him with her usual warm smile, the kind that could disarm anyone. She invited him inside, offered him tea, and spoke of the missing children with just the right amount of concern. "It's a tragedy," she said, her voice soft, "but children are always running away. It's just the way things are. People don't realize how lost they can feel sometimes."

Harris looked at her, trying to read her, trying to figure out if she was lying. But there was something in her eyes, a glint of something cold and distant, that made his stomach turn. He left after a few minutes, but not without a growing sense of dread.

Days passed, and the disappearances continued. Parents began to speak out, and the press picked up the story. The whispers grew louder. Maggie, however, kept her face calm and serene. She maintained her usual persona, never showing a hint of distress, never offering anything other than empathy and concern.

It wasn't until the final child, a girl named Lily, went missing that the truth finally came to light. Harris had followed Maggie one evening, shadowing her from a distance. He saw her walk to the front door of the family's home, and he knew something was wrong. He followed her to the park down the street, where she stopped and looked around, making sure no one was watching. That's when she met a man, a man Harris didn't recognize, and handed him something small wrapped in a cloth.

Harris moved closer, and what he saw made his blood run cold. The man took the cloth and unwrapped it, revealing Lily's stuffed animal—her favorite. The man smiled at Maggie and walked away. Harris rushed forward and tackled her to the ground.

"Where is she?" he demanded. "Where is Lily?"

Maggie didn't resist. She didn't even struggle. She just looked at him with the same serene expression that had fooled everyone for so long. "She's not the first," Maggie said, her voice calm, detached. "And she won't be the last."

When Harris found Lily's body hidden in a nearby shed, he understood the twisted truth. Maggie had been selecting the most neglected children, the ones no one would miss, the ones whose lives didn't matter to anyone except her. She had turned their desperation into a game, feeding off their need for comfort, and then disposing of them once she had used them for her own sick desires.

Maggie never spoke again after that. She never said why she had done it. But Harris realized too late—just like the parents, just like the children—he had been blind to what was happening right under his nose. The children had been neglected, but so had he. He had failed to see the darkness behind her smile.

The lesson, however, was clear. Some people prey on the weak, not because they want something from them, but because they can. And in the end, they leave nothing but silence behind.

The Golden Cage

Elena had always known what she wanted. She wasn't interested in love or companionship in the traditional sense. She had no illusions of romance, no desire for the fantasy so many women craved. She wanted power, stability, and comfort—the things she had never known as a young girl growing up in the neglected, dimly lit corners of the city. Wealthy men were the answer, and she knew how to play the game.

Her first marriage had been to a businessman in his fifties, a man whose fortune was vast but whose health was frail. She had courted him for months, feeding his ego and pretending to care for his every need. He had been charmed by her beauty and innocence, convinced that he had found the perfect wife—a young, gorgeous woman who adored him. But Elena's attention to detail was more calculating than affectionate. She knew how to make him feel like the only man in the room. And once she was married to him, once she was secure in his wealth, she began her plan.

Slowly, she introduced small amounts of poison into his diet, carefully calculating the dosage over weeks, then months. It wasn't quick or obvious—just enough to weaken him, to keep him sick, but not enough to raise suspicion. At first, it was the little things. A slightly bitter taste in his tea, a strange aftertaste in his soup. Over time, his energy began to fade. He complained of nausea and fatigue, his once robust frame shrinking before Elena's eyes. She was always there to care for him, to bring him his medication and soothe him when he felt unwell, all the while her true intentions hidden beneath a smile. His doctors couldn't figure out what was wrong, and neither could the rest of his family, who never visited enough to notice the changes.

By the time he passed, it had been so gradual that no one suspected foul play. Elena inherited his fortune, his vast estate, and his company. She sold the mansion, took the money, and moved on to her next target. She knew exactly what she was doing, and the routine was becoming almost second nature. The first man had been just a stepping stone—an introduction to the life she had always wanted. After him, there were others. There were always others.

Her second husband had been a widower in his early sixties, a kind man who doted on her like a queen. He was gentle, generous, and completely unaware of Elena's dark side. He treated her as if she were porcelain, something delicate and precious, while she saw him as little more than another vehicle for her rise. Once the wedding was over and the honeymoon faded into the background, Elena resumed her slow poisoning. She had become more skilled, more confident in her craft. She knew exactly what to do to weaken his body without raising any red flags. She did it all with the same calm demeanor, the same patient, loving care.

Her second husband's decline was even more drawn out than the first. It took longer this time, and Elena found herself almost bored by the process, her methodical patience giving way to a strange feeling of detached control. He spent his final days in a hospital bed, hooked up to tubes and machines, his once vibrant face gaunt and ashen. When he finally passed, the grief-stricken friends and family blamed his declining health on age, on his previous illness, on anything other than the woman who had been by his side all along. Elena was there for the funeral, dressed in black, a veil covering her face, the picture of widowhood.

The money poured in once again, and she couldn't help but smile as she watched it all fall into place. She had kept a small memento from each marriage—tiny trophies of her conquests. A ring from the first husband, a watch from the second. They were meaningless to her, of course. Just reminders of the price she had paid for security and power.

By the time she married her third husband, she had refined her techniques. This one was younger, more successful, and far more cautious. But Elena had always been able to charm the most guarded men. She knew how to make them feel special, how to appeal to their egos and their fears. And so, after months of careful courting, she was married again—this time to a wealthy entrepreneur who had built his fortune from the ground up. He had a young son, a child who adored his father and seemed to trust Elena instantly.

But this time, something was different. She hadn't planned on the boy, hadn't counted on how the child's presence would make her feel. He was always around, always underfoot, always watching. His innocent eyes followed her, his small, trusting hands reaching out for her when she passed by. Elena didn't know why it bothered her so much, but it did. She found herself increasingly irritated by his presence, by his neediness, by the way he looked at her as though she were something other than the woman who had come into their lives to destroy it.

As time went on, Elena's usual routine continued. She made the drinks, prepared the meals, watched her husband's health slowly decline in the same way she had with the others. But there was a twist this time. The boy, despite his innocence, began to notice the small things. He watched her prepare the drinks, listened to the way she spoke to his father. Elena had been too careful before, too confident in her ability to cover her tracks, but this time, there was a nagging feeling in the back of her mind that she couldn't shake.

One night, the boy found a hidden drawer in the study, tucked away under some old papers. Inside were the trophies—her rings, her watches, the objects that represented the lives she had taken. He took them to his father, who confronted Elena, shocked by the realization of what she had done.

For the first time, Elena felt a flicker of fear. Her husband was on the verge of calling the police, of ending her reign of terror, when the boy's voice broke the silence.

"Mommy, please don't let her do this again," the child said softly, eyes wide with both innocence and terror.

Her husband, already frail and confused from the slow poison Elena had been feeding him, looked at the boy, the realization dawning on him too late.

But Elena didn't panic. She didn't flinch. With one swift motion, she reached into her purse and pulled out the final dose.

This time, it wasn't for her husband.

Elena smiled coldly as she watched the boy slump to the floor, his innocent eyes dimming forever. Her husband never saw it coming.

The lesson, though it was lost on her, was clear. Elena had been so focused on building her empire of wealth and control that she had overlooked the one thing that could have brought her down. A child's unspoken trust, a pure love, had been the thing that shattered her illusion of invincibility. In the end, the trophies she kept would be her only company, and she would die as alone as the first man she had poisoned, always searching for more.

The Lesson in Pain

Rachel Harmon had always been an excellent teacher. She was well-liked by her students and respected by her colleagues. For years, she had poured her life into shaping young minds, believing in the transformative power of education. But beneath her carefully crafted exterior, a darkness festered—one that had grown over time, nurtured by her frustrations with a system that seemed to fail those who needed it most.

It started with one student, Jason. He was a troubled kid, the kind who always seemed to be in the principal's office or under the scrutiny of the guidance counselor. His grades were slipping, his attitude was defiant, and he had a general disdain for authority. To most teachers, he was a lost cause, a kid who would never amount to much. But Rachel saw something different. She saw him as a challenge, a puzzle she could solve—a chance to prove that her methods could work where others had failed.

She began to pay special attention to him. She would linger after class, asking him questions about his life, his interests, his troubles. At first, Jason resisted, shrugging her off with sarcasm, but Rachel was persistent. She understood him in ways that no one else seemed to. She knew that his anger wasn't just a rebellion against authority—it was a cry for help. And Rachel, ever the nurturer, believed she could fix him.

She started giving him extra assignments, keeping him after school to talk. Her words were soft, but they carried a weight—one that drew him in. She told him she believed in him, that he had potential, that he was more than the sum of his mistakes. Slowly, Jason began to soften. His grades improved, he started to attend class regularly, and for the first time in a long time, he seemed to believe that someone cared.

But Rachel didn't stop there. She needed more. She needed to see how far she could push him, how far she could manipulate his emotions to see just how much control she had. She wanted to see if she could break him down completely and rebuild him in her image. It was an experiment—a twisted, dark experiment. She had been a teacher long enough to know that some students were beyond saving, but Jason had come too close. He was her project now, and she couldn't let him slip through her fingers.

The conversations grew more intense. Rachel began to probe deeper, asking about his family, his relationships, his struggles. She knew about the broken home, the absent father, the mother who was always too busy or too drunk to care. But Rachel, ever the manipulator, acted as if she could be the one to fill the void. She told him things—things that no teacher should tell a student. She told him that he was special, that they shared a connection no one else would understand. And she told him she could save him—if only he would let her.

Jason began to trust her. It was all too easy. But Rachel had no intention of saving him. She wasn't trying to help him overcome his demons. No, she was playing a much darker game. She needed him to need her, to depend on her so completely that he would lose himself in her control. She pushed him further, exploiting his vulnerabilities. She made him question his worth, made him believe that without her, he would fall apart. And when he did, when he broke under the pressure of his own self-doubt, Rachel was there to pick up the pieces.

But it wasn't enough. Jason wasn't enough. She needed more. She needed to see if she could do it with others—if she could replicate her success, her control, on a wider scale. She began to pick her next targets, students who, like Jason, were lost causes. She chose those who seemed beyond saving, those who had no support at home, those who carried visible scars—emotional and physical—that no one cared to acknowledge. Each one became part of her experiment, each one a new challenge to overcome.

Her methods became more refined over time. She would target the weakest students, the ones who needed attention the most. She would provide that attention, pretending to be their ally, their friend, their confidant. She would listen to their stories, their pain, and offer advice—advice that was often laced with manipulation. She would tell them that they didn't need anyone else, that they could rely on her. And just as with Jason, she pushed them further, exploiting their emotional and physical weaknesses, seeing how far they would bend before they broke.

And break they did. One by one, Rachel's students crumbled under the weight of her false promises, their lives spiraling out of control. They stopped attending school, their grades plummeted, and some of them even started skipping class altogether. But Rachel didn't care. She wasn't interested in their success. She wasn't interested in their well-being. She only wanted to see how much they would give her, how much she could strip away before they were no longer able to function on their own.

One day, after a particularly intense session with one of her students, a young girl named Lily, Rachel realized just how far she had gone. Lily had come to her for help, but what Rachel had done was so much darker. She had told Lily that she could be someone, that she was beautiful, that she didn't need anyone else but Rachel to guide her. She had told her all the things Lily had wanted to hear, knowing that her words would ensnare her. And Lily had believed her. She had given herself over to Rachel completely, and Rachel had exploited it. She had taken everything from Lily—the girl's self-worth, her sense of identity—and in return, she had promised her nothing but destruction.

The next day, Rachel didn't see Lily in class. It wasn't unusual for some students to skip, but something about the empty chair unsettled her. It wasn't until the end of the day that she heard the news. Lily had gone missing. The police were involved, a search was underway, but

Rachel didn't feel the panic that everyone else did. In fact, she felt a strange sense of calm. She knew where Lily was. She had seen the way the girl had slipped away, the way she had been so easily manipulated.

But it wasn't until the police arrived at her door, until they asked her questions about Lily, that Rachel realized the extent of her obsession. She had gone too far. She had crossed a line that could never be uncrossed. The twisted satisfaction she had once felt in controlling her students, in making them believe she could save them, was now a prison she could never escape from. She had fed off their pain, and now she was trapped in her own web of lies.

As Rachel was led away in handcuffs, she looked back at the classroom—the place she had once felt so powerful, so invincible. But now it felt hollow, empty. The lesson had been taught, but it was not one she could ever escape. And in the end, there would be no redemption, no second chance for her, only the cold, unforgiving truth that she had been the true "lost cause" all along.

The Last Course

Isabella had always been known for her charm. A striking woman with a captivating smile and a warm, easy demeanor, she made an instant impression wherever she went. Her natural grace and her ability to make people feel comfortable in her presence had earned her a reputation as the most pleasant person in the kitchen of *Le Jardin d'Or*, an upscale restaurant that catered to the city's elite.

She had worked her way up from the bottom, from a simple prep cook to a line chef. Her skill with food was undeniable—every dish she created seemed to melt in the mouth, an orchestra of flavors that kept customers coming back for more. She wasn't the head chef, but she didn't need to be. Isabella knew her worth, and the patrons knew it too. The regulars would come into the restaurant just for her creations, asking for her by name. There was always something magnetic about Isabella's food—it wasn't just the flavors, it was the way she made them feel. People felt seen when they ate her dishes, and she prided herself on that.

But it wasn't just her culinary talents that made her special. It was the way she carried herself, the way she always listened when others spoke, the way she made them feel like the most important person in the room. That was her gift. She made people feel noticed and valued, and for the longest time, she had thought it was enough. But over the years, Isabella had come to understand something about herself—something she couldn't ignore.

Some people were ungrateful.

Some people took without giving back, without ever recognizing what she had done for them. And in the kitchen, that feeling of being overlooked was something she experienced regularly. She had put in the long hours, the extra shifts, the overtime, but it was always the same few who received the praise. Always the same people who basked in the glory of the restaurant's success, while Isabella worked in the shadows, creating the magic behind the scenes. She had given them everything—the best dishes, the secret ingredients, the tricks of the trade—but no one had ever acknowledged her, at least not in the way she deserved.

It started subtly at first. A little too much salt here, a dash of something unidentifiable there. A drop of something that made the food just a little too bitter or a little too rich. It was all part of the craft, a way to take control of her surroundings when the system seemed stacked against her. After all, she had seen the way the head chef, Richard, took credit for her work, the way the sous-chefs ignored her ideas, the way customers fawned over the dishes without ever knowing the name behind them. She was tired of being invisible. She was tired of playing the role of the quiet, obedient chef.

And so, it began.

She started small—an extra spice in a vinaigrette that would upset the stomach, a rare herb that made the fish just a little too rich for comfort. She knew how much to use, just enough to make people uncomfortable but not enough to cause suspicion. Her coworkers began to notice the strange mix of flavors, the odd aftertaste, but no one said anything. After all, everyone was busy. The kitchen was loud, chaotic, and fast-paced. No one had time to stop and question a slightly off dish.

But Isabella's confidence grew with each success. No one questioned her. She was still the charming, talented cook they all relied on, but now she had a new power—a power over them that she wasn't ready to give up. Her growing resentment began to seep into her food, adding something more than just the usual seasonings. She found herself giving a little more than just extra salt. A drop of something more lethal, something with a slow burn. Something she had learned about in a quiet corner of the kitchen, hidden in the space where the herbs and oils met.

Richard was the first. She had always loathed his smug smile, his tendency to take credit for her ideas. It was a particularly busy night, a group of VIPs from out of town were in, and the pressure was mounting. Richard called for a perfect risotto, and Isabella had already prepped the ingredients—her recipe, her work—but he insisted on changing the seasoning. He said it needed something extra. And she gave it to him. Just a pinch of something she'd learned about—a subtle poison that was tasteless, odorless, and that took its toll over hours. By the time Richard started to feel it, he was already too far gone. He tried to hide it, of course, but he couldn't. His stomach churned. He went pale, and by the end of the night, he collapsed in the back office. No one suspected anything more than food poisoning. A few days later, Richard was gone, blamed for his poor health and bad decisions.

Then came the others—Kelly, the sous-chef, who had undermined her at every turn, taking credit for ideas she had given her; Marcus, the waiter, who had been so flirtatious with her in a way that always made her uncomfortable; and a few of the other kitchen staff who had grown so complacent in their own importance that they forgot where their food came from. One by one, she picked them off, using her charm and her food to slowly, subtly erase them from the restaurant.

It wasn't just the coworkers. It was the customers too—the ones who had praised her food, but never bothered to ask for her name. They were just as guilty. She didn't target them all, but the ones who had forgotten her, the ones who had treated her as a mere accessory to the experience, became her targets. A little extra something in their dessert, a subtle touch to their drink that left them weaker by the hour. It was her revenge, her way of taking back control.

But then, one evening, something unexpected happened. A new critic came to dine, a food writer who had heard the whispers of *Le Jardin d'Or*'s latest culinary star. The critic was intrigued by the dishes, intrigued by the flavors, and especially intrigued by the chef behind them. Isabella was finally noticed—not just as a part of the machine, but as the heart of it. The critic asked for her name, and for the first time in years, Isabella felt a flutter of hope. Finally, someone would know the truth. Finally, she would be recognized for the work she had done.

But as she walked into the dining room to meet the critic, she saw the plates, the desserts, and something inside her twisted. The critic had ordered the exact same dishes that had been poisoned—the ones that had already begun to take their toll. She realized with a cold rush that in her haste, in her need for validation, she had overplayed her hand.

The critic tasted her food and died before the night was over, his body succumbing to the poison before the restaurant could react. Isabella's work was done, but not the way she had intended. The recognition she so desperately craved was now overshadowed by the horror of her own creations. In the end, it wasn't her talent or her charm that would define her legacy, but the deaths she had caused, the lives she had destroyed in her quest for power. Her brilliance had been her undoing, and the restaurant she had loved would never remember her as the chef she dreamed of being, but as the poisoner who took everything too far.

Isabella's charm had seduced many, but in the end, it was the very thing that led to her downfall. It was a lesson she would never get to learn.

Behind Closed Doors

Carla Miller was the perfect mother. At least, that's what everyone thought. The neighbors saw her each morning, waving at them as she drove her kids off to school, a soft smile on her face, a polished appearance that hid any trace of her darker side. She spent her days cleaning the house, organizing, running errands, and attending PTA meetings—always with a pleasant, composed demeanor. To anyone who observed, she had the life they all dreamed of: a beautiful home, a loving husband, two well-behaved children, and a life that seemed effortlessly perfect.

But behind the façade of her picture-perfect existence, Carla harbored a secret. Her home was her prison, and she lived with a quiet, simmering jealousy toward the women around her who seemed to have it all together. The women who were better mothers, who had more successful careers, who made her feel small with their shiny, perfect lives. Carla was exhausted by her own perceived failures, convinced that she could never live up to the impossible standards set by those around her. And so, in the darkest corners of her mind, she began to fantasize.

It started with Angela, her neighbor across the street. Angela had two children, but somehow she managed to always appear put-together—her clothes were fashionable, her house immaculate, and she balanced her job and family life with an ease Carla couldn't comprehend. Angela's kids were always happy and polite, her husband doted on her, and she was constantly involved in charity work. To Carla, Angela seemed like the embodiment of everything she wasn't. And every time she saw her, that quiet resentment grew.

At first, it was just thoughts, harmless and fleeting. But soon, Carla began to notice the little things—the way Angela would chat about her career, her children's accomplishments, the trips they'd taken, the way people looked at her with admiration. Carla saw Angela's life as everything hers wasn't, and the more she saw it, the more she began to loathe her. But what could Carla do? Her own life felt like it was slipping through her fingers, and she could barely keep up with her responsibilities. Angela was the perfect mother, the perfect woman. And Carla had had enough.

One night, after a PTA meeting, Carla saw Angela out in her yard, tending to her flowers. The perfect picture of domestic bliss, smiling as she watered her rose bushes, humming a cheerful tune. Carla stood at her window, watching her, her chest tight with envy. She could feel her pulse quicken, her breath growing shallow as a dark thought crossed her mind. *What if Angela was just a little less perfect? What if, just for a moment, the pressure of all her achievements could vanish?*

The thought grew. Carla knew it wasn't rational, but in the quiet of her own home, in the silence of her own mind, it felt like the only solution to her misery.

And so, Carla began to plan. She'd noticed Angela's weakness—her habit of drinking a glass of wine at dinner every evening. It was a harmless indulgence, something Carla had never paid much attention to. But now, in the dark recesses of her mind, it became a weapon. She knew Angela had a habit of leaving the wine bottle on the counter after a pour, the same place she left the bottle each evening. All Carla needed was to slip something into it. Something that would take the edge off her perfect life, something that would push Angela to the brink.

It wasn't difficult. Carla had done her research, learned about the effects of a particular combination of pills—sedatives that could be undetectable if used carefully, pills that would cause drowsiness and confusion. Over the next week, Carla followed Angela's movements, memorized the exact time she opened the bottle, and then, one night, she slipped the pills in. It was subtle, like everything Carla did—nothing overt, nothing that could be traced back to her. She waited, and as the evening wore on, she saw Angela stagger back into the house, her steps unsteady, her face flushed with the effects of the drugs.

The next day, Angela didn't show up for the school carpool. Carla smiled to herself, but it was short-lived. Over the next few days, she watched as Angela's life began to spiral. She couldn't quite put her finger on it, but something was off. Angela's perfect smile faltered, her kids started acting up, and she began to look tired, like something had drained the life out of her. The whole neighborhood began to notice the change. Carla watched from the sidelines, a sense of satisfaction growing inside her.

But as the days passed, Carla realized that Angela's deterioration wasn't enough. The damage wasn't deep enough. Angela wasn't falling apart fast enough. Carla wanted more. She needed more. And so, with a twisted sense of finality, Carla made the decision. She would push Angela even further, create a crisis that would ruin her once and for all. She could sense it—the tipping point, where Angela's life would break into a million pieces. It wouldn't take much more. A few more carefully placed pills, a nudge in the right direction.

But something strange happened. Angela's behavior didn't continue to worsen. In fact, after a few days, Angela began to stabilize. She was still exhausted, still seemed off, but she was getting better. She started to return to her routines. Her children, once wild with confusion, began to settle down. Angela was regaining control. And with that, Carla felt a flicker of panic. Her plan was unraveling.

Then one day, Angela came over to Carla's house. It was unexpected, a knock on the door while Carla was folding laundry. She answered it with a smile, her heart racing, but the perfect mask was still in place.

"I just wanted to thank you," Angela said softly, stepping into the living room. "For everything. I don't know what happened, but I've felt so... out of sorts lately. I've been so distracted and worried, but I think I finally figured it out. My daughter found the pills I've been taking—the ones I've been mixing with the wine—and she confronted me. I didn't even realize it. I've been going through some personal stuff, and I just didn't know how to cope. I'm sorry if I've seemed off."

Carla's blood ran cold. The pills. They weren't even her doing. Angela had been sabotaging herself all along. Her perfect life had been cracking under pressure for reasons Carla had never understood. The weight of the secret she had kept from everyone had been too much for Angela to carry, and without Carla's interference, she had already been breaking down.

Carla felt a wave of nausea sweep over her as the truth hit her—the very thing she had thought was her revenge, her victory, was a figment of her own imagination. Angela hadn't been the problem. Carla had been projecting her own insecurities, her own rage at not being good enough. The jealousy, the hatred she felt toward Angela had blinded her to the reality. Angela's life hadn't been perfect at all. It was just like everyone else's—full of pain, full of struggle, and full of failure.

And as Angela left, her back turned to Carla's disbelieving gaze, Carla was left standing in the doorway, finally seeing the cracks in her own perfect world. She had nearly destroyed someone else to feel better about herself, and in the process, she had almost lost everything.

The Black Veil

Mara had always been different. From a young age, she gravitated toward the darkness—toward the poetry of Edgar Allan Poe, the melancholic lyrics of Siouxsie Sioux, and the haunting fashion that screamed rebellion against the mundane. She dressed in black, wore heavy eyeliner, and adorned herself with silver jewelry that seemed to echo the whispers of the forgotten. To the world, she was just another goth girl in a sea of black—misunderstood and quietly standing apart. But what the world didn't know was that Mara's world was ruled by a set of strict, unyielding rules.

The goth subculture had meant everything to her once. It was where she found her identity, her solace from a world that never seemed to understand. She believed in the power of darkness, in individuality, and in rejecting the hollow norms of society. But over the years, as she immersed herself deeper into the scene, she began to notice something unsettling. It wasn't the world that had failed her—it was the very subculture she had held so dear. The people who claimed to embrace the same ideals, the ones who called themselves "true goths," seemed to be nothing more than posers, shallow in their pursuit of a trend that had long since lost its meaning. They wore the clothes but lacked the heart. They wore the makeup but had no understanding of the darkness they pretended to represent.

Mara became disillusioned. The scene had become a mockery, a parody of what it once stood for. Her friends—if they could even be called that—were the worst offenders. They sought attention more than authenticity, flaunting their outfits in clubs and posting selfies online, seeking likes and approval like everyone else. They were nothing more than children playing dress-up, hiding behind the veil of darkness while living in the light of shallow vanity. They spoke of being outsiders, but their actions showed they had long since abandoned the very principles that made them different.

Mara couldn't stand it any longer. She had tried to change them—tried to shake them awake. But nothing worked. The betrayal she felt cut deeper with each passing day, and soon, her disgust turned into something darker. If they weren't going to honor the subculture, if they weren't going to respect the darkness that had once saved them, then they deserved to be punished. She would cleanse the scene. She would make them pay for their betrayal.

It began with Lily, a girl she had once called a friend. Lily was a self-proclaimed goth, always posting pictures of herself dressed in tight black clothing and heavy makeup. But Mara knew better. Lily's world was one of Instagram filters and empty, hollow words. She was nothing more than a vain little girl playing at being dark. Mara had watched her for months, seeing her flaunt her so-called "goth" lifestyle, yet all she did was chase the approval of others, desperate for attention. Her soul was as empty as the lights of her phone screen.

The night Lily was found dead, her body sprawled on the floor of her apartment, no one suspected foul play. To the untrained eye, it was a tragic overdose, an unfortunate misstep in the fragile, chaotic world of youth. But to Mara, it was a necessary sacrifice—a cleansing of the subculture. The ritual was simple. She had drugged Lily's drink just enough to make her slip into unconsciousness, then covered her body in ritualistic symbols, symbols she had learned from years of reading ancient, forgotten texts. She didn't just kill Lily; she *purified* her. The knife she used wasn't just for the physical act. It was to sever the false pretenses, to cleanse Lily of her superficiality. A final offering to the darkness that had once been pure.

Mara felt a strange sense of satisfaction afterward, the act of purging the scene of what it no longer deserved. She watched as the goth community mourned Lily, never suspecting the true cause of her death. The self-righteous pity of her so-called friends only made Mara's resolve stronger. But she couldn't stop there. The work wasn't finished. There were more to cleanse.

It wasn't long before Mara turned her eyes on the others. Next came Greg, a boy who, like Lily, pretended to belong but whose heart was made of empty promises and half-formed ideals. He was always at the clubs, always posing, always seeking attention. He was the type of person who would claim to embrace darkness, but his heart was nothing more than a shallow vessel searching for validation. Greg had ruined the meaning of goth in a way that Mara could no longer tolerate. So, she followed him for weeks, learning his patterns, waiting for the right moment to strike.

Mara found him one evening at a local bar, drunk and boasting about his latest conquests. He wore the uniform, but he had no respect for the values that came with it. He laughed at the music, mocked the poetry, and belittled those who actually lived the lifestyle he pretended to embody. She didn't hesitate. She knew what she had to do. She slipped something into his drink—something that would slow his heart, make him weak and compliant. She led him out of the bar, away from the prying eyes of the world. There, in the dark alley, she made him pay for his hypocrisy. His death, like Lily's, was another sacrifice—another necessary step to return purity to the subculture that had been twisted beyond recognition.

By now, the goth community was in turmoil, whispers of tragedies and accidents circulating through the bars and clubs, but no one connected the dots. The deaths were just another part of the chaos, the recklessness of youth. But to Mara, they were her rituals, her redemption. She had become something more than just a girl in black clothes. She was a savior of the scene, an executioner who would rid the world of those who didn't deserve it. The darkness was hers to command.

Then, one night, she met Clara, a new arrival to the goth community. Clara was everything Mara had once been—a true believer in the ideals, someone who lived the life with honesty and authenticity. She didn't care about followers or likes. Clara was the purity Mara had been searching for. For the first time in months, Mara felt a pang of doubt. Clara had earned her place in the community. She was one of the few who truly embodied the ideals that Mara had once held dear.

But as the days went on, Clara began to change. She became more popular, more visible. She started attending more events, making connections with the very people Mara despised. Clara's authenticity was replaced with a growing need for attention, for validation. The purity Mara had once seen in her began to fade, replaced by the same shallow behaviors that had marked the others.

Mara knew what had to be done.

The night of Clara's death, Mara felt a sickening sense of finality. She had done what she set out to do—cleansed the subculture of its impure elements. But as she watched Clara's lifeless body in front of her, the final ritual complete, Mara realized something that made her stomach churn with horror: She had become the very thing she despised. She had betrayed the ideals she once claimed to protect, twisted them into something dark and unrecognizable. Her obsession with purity had consumed her, and now, there was no escape.

The lesson was clear, though it was too late for Mara to learn it. In her zeal to punish others for their betrayal, she had become the ultimate hypocrite. In seeking to purify the goth subculture, she had destroyed herself. And in the end, the darkness that had once saved her had become her prison.

Tame the Beast

Carly had always loved animals. From the time she could remember, she had been surrounded by them. Her childhood was filled with the comforting presence of cats, birds, and, especially, dogs. There was something about the way animals looked at her—so trusting, so utterly dependent—that brought her a sense of power. She had always enjoyed the feeling of being in control. She made sure to feed them, to clean their cages, to walk them and teach them tricks. But, at night, she liked to watch them squirm beneath her gaze, the way they hesitated, the way they could never truly understand her. It was when they were weak, when they were at their most vulnerable, that she felt her power fully ignite.

At first, her cruelty had been subtle. She would tug too hard on the leash, squeeze a bit too tightly around a dog's neck as she brushed its fur. When her pets misbehaved, she wouldn't hesitate to strike them, leaving marks that only she could see. She wasn't always malicious. Most of the time, she genuinely enjoyed their companionship. But something inside her was growing darker. She started to wonder—just how far could she push them before they broke? How much control could she wield before they became nothing more than an extension of her will?

Her first real test came when she adopted Max, a large, stubborn terrier mix. He was a beautiful dog, full of energy and defiance, and he quickly became the target of Carly's need for dominance. She would make him sit for hours, barely acknowledging him as he shifted uncomfortably at her feet. She would withhold food for days at a time, then reward him with scraps, just enough to keep him begging for more. She saw him as an experiment, a tool to feed her growing obsession.

But one evening, Max made a fatal mistake. After days of forced obedience and hunger, he snapped. He growled at her, a low, guttural sound that sent a thrill down her spine. For a moment, the world seemed to pause as she looked into his eyes. He had betrayed her. The beast she had kept on a tight leash had finally shown its true colors. She could see the rebellion, the wildness in him that no amount of training could suppress. The terror of his defiance caused a wave of fury to crash over her.

Without thinking, Carly grabbed a knife from the kitchen, the cold steel glinting under the dim light of the room. Max's bark echoed in her ears as she raised the blade. She told herself it was just a moment of weakness, a final act of control. She had to do this—she had to show him who was in charge. She drove the knife into his side, watching in both horror and fascination as he crumpled to the floor.

The blood was warm and sticky as it pooled around his body. Carly stared at him, her heart pounding, her breath shallow, but something inside her clicked. This wasn't fear. This was power. The taste of control was intoxicating, and she realized that she wasn't just taking out her frustration on an animal. She had crossed a line, one she could never uncross.

From that moment on, Carly's needs grew more intense. She couldn't stop at dogs. Her thirst for control began to seep into other areas of her life. It wasn't long before she started targeting the people around her—the ones she felt could be manipulated, the ones who were too trusting, too willing to be led. It was subtle at first. A few random acquaintances here and there, those she thought could disappear without anyone noticing. She found a sense of satisfaction in watching them unravel beneath her influence, testing their limits, pushing them to the brink before she discarded them, much like she had discarded her pets.

It was Claire, however, who became Carly's true obsession. Claire was new to the neighborhood, an artist with soft eyes and a shy demeanor. She had adopted a rescue dog from the shelter, a young golden retriever named Bella. Carly's need to control grew sharper as she watched Claire's relationship with Bella flourish. It wasn't just the dog—it was the connection. Carly couldn't stand how freely Claire gave her heart to someone else. She couldn't stand that, despite all of her manipulation, Claire still seemed to possess something Carly could never have: a deep, unconditional bond with another living being.

Carly's jealousy grew poisonous, a festering sore inside her. She watched as Claire and Bella walked in the park every day, laughing together, sharing moments of tenderness. Carly would drive by them in her car, feeling the heat of envy rise in her chest. She couldn't bear it anymore. She had to destroy it.

One day, she approached Claire under the pretense of offering help with her dog, telling her she had experience with training. Claire was hesitant but grateful. Carly offered to take Bella for a walk, to help her burn off some energy. It was too easy. Claire trusted her, like all the others had.

Carly took the dog and walked her to a secluded area near a wooded park, far enough away that no one could see them. She tightened the leash, leading Bella deeper into the shadows. The dog whimpered but followed obediently. Carly's hands shook with excitement as she imagined the look on Claire's face when she learned what had happened, when she realized that even her beloved pet had been stolen from her.

Carly stood there, her breath quickening as Bella tried to wriggle free from her grip. She had been through this before. She knew exactly what she had to do. She pulled the leash tighter, watching as Bella gasped for breath. The control she felt as the life slowly drained from the dog's body was unlike anything she had experienced before. This wasn't just an animal. This was a message, a way to show Claire how insignificant her world was to Carly, how easy it was to break it apart.

When the dog finally stopped moving, Carly stood over her, the leash still in her hand. She stared at Bella's lifeless body, her chest heaving, the adrenaline rush subsiding into an eerie calm. She had done it again. She had taken something pure, something beautiful, and twisted it for her own satisfaction. But as she walked back to Claire's house, a nagging thought tugged at her—something she hadn't anticipated. What would Claire do? What would she say?

When Carly arrived at the door, Claire was waiting. There was a nervous energy about her, but there was no sign of the dog. "Is Bella with you?" Claire asked, her voice filled with uncertainty.

Carly opened her mouth, but the words caught in her throat. She couldn't lie—she couldn't bring herself to say the words. Claire's eyes searched hers for any hint of what had happened, but Carly remained silent. Finally, Claire's face fell, a shadow passing over her features. She turned, her shoulders shaking as the truth hung heavy in the air.

The shock of Claire's reaction hit Carly harder than she expected. She had destroyed everything. But this time, it wasn't just a dog she had killed. It was the last part of herself that could ever feel human.

In the end, Carly realized the truth too late: The power she had craved was never truly hers to control. The violence, the manipulation, the destruction—none of it had ever given her what she wanted. All it had done was make her feel emptier, more isolated. The beast she thought she could tame had consumed her.

The Crimson Circle

Miriam had always been good at reading people. It was a skill she had honed over the years, as a child trying to win her parents' approval and later, as an adult navigating the complexities of human interaction. She knew how to charm people, how to make them believe she understood them in ways no one else could. It was this skill that led her to start her small, secretive group—a gathering of like-minded individuals who sought something greater, something beyond the mundanity of everyday life.

It began innocently enough. Miriam was an intellectual, well-read in philosophy, religion, and ancient texts. She believed deeply in the concept of enlightenment, in the idea that true power could only be attained through sacrifice and transformation. Over time, she attracted others—vulnerable people who felt lost, who longed for purpose. She fed them ideas, told them they were part of something bigger than themselves, and slowly, she wove a web of loyalty and devotion. Her words were honey, dripping with the promise of answers to all their questions, all their fears. Miriam knew how to make them feel special, how to convince them that they were chosen, that they were meant for greatness.

At first, the group was small—a handful of people who met in secret, who shared their dreams and their ambitions. They called themselves *The Crimson Circle*. To them, it was an exclusive club, a sanctuary from the outside world. Miriam promised them that through her teachings, they could transcend their human limitations and become something more. She spoke of spiritual awakening, of cleansing the world of its impurities, of reaching a higher plane where only the worthy would ascend.

But as the weeks went by, Miriam began to push them further. She asked them to let go of their attachments—to their families, their friends, their possessions. "Sacrifice is the path to purity," she would say. "Only through shedding the old can we embrace the new." Her followers, eager to please, complied. They abandoned their old lives, disconnected from the world they once knew, and devoted themselves entirely to her. They believed they were serving a higher purpose, that their sacrifices would lead them to the answers they had sought for so long.

And then, one night, Miriam made her request. It was subtle at first, a suggestion wrapped in the guise of spiritual enlightenment. "To truly transcend," she said, "we must prove our commitment. We must rid ourselves of the filth that clings to this world, the impurities that hinder our ascension." Her followers nodded, their eyes wide with anticipation. Miriam had always been careful with her words, making sure each one landed with the weight of inevitability.

"One must give more than just material possessions," she continued. "We must give of ourselves—our very being. We must offer up that which is most sacred, most pure, to cleanse the world."

The first sacrifice came soon after. Miriam told them that a man, a man she had identified as corrupt and vile, was an obstacle to their mission. He was a business tycoon, a man whose name Miriam had heard in passing. He symbolized everything that was wrong with the world—a symbol of greed, corruption, and self-interest. She told them it was necessary, that his death would free them from his toxic influence. She spoke of it as if it were a simple matter of purification.

Her followers did not hesitate. They trusted her completely, their loyalty unquestioned. It was as if they had been waiting for the moment to act, to prove their devotion to the cause. Miriam led them to the man's house, a mansion perched on a hill, isolated and vulnerable. They broke in, and Miriam orchestrated the entire event with a cold precision. The man was killed quickly, his life snuffed out as though it were nothing more than a passing shadow.

The group celebrated that night, feeling a rush of power as they watched the news reports about the businessman's death. Miriam assured them that it was only the beginning. The act had been necessary, part of the plan. And as they looked at her with awe, they felt that they were becoming something more. They were shedding their humanity, embracing the darkness Miriam promised would bring them closer to the truth.

As time went on, the killings became more frequent, more brutal. Miriam's control over the group tightened. She would tell them that each sacrifice was a step closer to achieving their ultimate goal. She convinced them that they had a duty to rid the world of those who were unworthy, to cleanse the earth of its impurities. And so, they killed again and again—people they deemed corrupt, people who had hurt them in some way, or simply those who no longer fit into the world they were creating.

But Miriam was not content with simply ridding the world of unworthy individuals. She wanted more. She craved power—absolute control. The group, once united in its devotion to the cause, began to fracture. Some of the followers grew uneasy, questioning Miriam's methods, wondering if the bloodshed was truly necessary. Miriam saw this as a threat to her authority, a challenge to her reign. She knew she had to act quickly, before anyone could turn against her.

The final sacrifice came swiftly. Miriam told them that one of their own—Emma, a young woman who had once been so devoted—had betrayed the group. Emma had begun to question Miriam's teachings, to voice doubts about the legitimacy of the murders. Miriam, sensing the weakness in Emma, made her the target of the ultimate act of devotion.

She gathered the group together, each one wearing the same blank expression of unquestioning loyalty. Emma was brought into the circle, her face pale with fear. Miriam spoke of purity, of sacrifice, of the need to remove all threats to their mission. The followers, their minds clouded by the years of manipulation, stood silently as Miriam took the knife.

But as she raised the blade, Emma's eyes met hers—not with fear, but with something else. A calmness, an understanding. She spoke softly, her voice carrying across the room. "Miriam, you're not doing this for us. You're doing it for you."

Miriam hesitated, the blade hovering over Emma's chest. The group remained still, waiting for her to act, but for the first time, Miriam felt a flicker of doubt. Was Emma right? Had she truly been guiding them toward something greater, or was she just using them to fulfill her own twisted desires? The question lingered in the air, thick with the weight of betrayal and realization.

But before Miriam could answer, one of her followers—a man named Caleb—lunged at her. In the chaos, the knife slipped from her hand, and Emma's voice echoed in Miriam's mind: *"You've already sacrificed everything. You've become the very thing you feared."*

In the end, Miriam realized too late that she had been the true sacrifice all along. Her thirst for power, her need for control, had led her down a path of destruction, and in the final moment, she understood that she had destroyed not just those she had killed, but herself as well.

The Sweetest Poison

Catherine Taylor was the perfect mother. At least, that's what everyone in her small suburban neighborhood thought. Her house was immaculate, her children well-behaved, and her husband, James, had the air of someone who was truly loved and admired. Catherine wore her caring persona like a badge of honor—always the first to volunteer for school fundraisers, always the one to bake cookies for the neighbors, always the one to offer a helping hand. The kind of woman who made everyone feel comfortable, reassured, and safe.

But beneath her radiant smile, something was slowly decaying.

She had always wanted the perfect family—the picture-perfect life with two children, a loving husband, and a beautiful home. But as the years wore on, Catherine began to realize that her perfect family wasn't perfect at all. James, though a good man, was distant, caught up in his work, consumed by the pressures of his job and the constant push to provide more. He was kind, but it wasn't enough. Her children, Emily and Nathan, were unruly at times, needing attention, but there was a sense that they would never truly understand the depths of her sacrifices. They took everything for granted, and she felt unnoticed, unappreciated. And so, in the quiet corners of her mind, she began to think.

Perhaps she could make them *better*. Perhaps she could show them a new life, a new peace.

Catherine began with small doses, careful and calculated. It was all for their own good, she convinced herself. Just a little something to make them more docile, more peaceful. She started with James. He drank a cup of tea every night before bed, a simple routine that had long since lost its charm. Catherine had always kept the tea cupboard stocked with herbal blends, teas designed for relaxation. But one day, she added a bit of something extra to James's cup—a slow-acting sedative that would help him sleep more deeply, more soundly. He complained the next morning of feeling groggy, but Catherine reassured him, telling him it was probably just the stress of work catching up with him. And it worked. His sleep improved. He was more relaxed, more pleasant, and though he didn't quite realize it, he grew more dependent on her care.

With James settled, Catherine turned her attention to her children. Emily, at fourteen, was the typical teenager—moody, rebellious, and always on her phone. Nathan, at ten, was a sweet boy but often got into trouble, testing boundaries and disobeying her every now and then. Catherine wasn't unloving—no, far from it. She cared for them deeply, but she couldn't help but feel frustrated by how little they seemed to appreciate her sacrifices. She had given them everything—the perfect home, the best education, all the love they could possibly need. But they still seemed so... ungrateful. So, once again, Catherine took matters into her own hands.

At first, it was just vitamins. She made them all breakfast each morning, slipping small doses of the poison she had researched into their orange juice or oatmeal. Nothing too dramatic, just enough to weaken them gradually, to make them tired and sluggish, to make them more dependent on her. It was all for their own good, of course. To protect them from the stresses of the world, to ensure they remained safe within the warm cocoon of her love.

But as the weeks passed, Catherine found herself growing more brazen. The doses increased, more frequent, more potent. She began to notice a shift in them—her children became quieter, less demanding, their energy ebbing away. Emily, once so defiant, now stayed in her room more, barely leaving except for meals. Nathan's once insatiable curiosity turned into lethargy. He would often fall asleep on the couch, his eyes half-lidded, too tired to run and play with his friends. But Catherine didn't mind. They were becoming what she wanted—obedient, calm, docile. James too was growing more and more pliable, more passive. He no longer argued with her when she suggested things, no longer resisted when she decided things for the family. The house was more peaceful than it had ever been.

As the weeks turned into months, Catherine's grip on her family tightened, but she didn't feel the guilt she thought she would. Instead, she felt relief. They were no longer a source of stress in her life. She could finally control everything—she could make sure they were happy, make sure they were safe, make sure they stayed with her forever in their little bubble. Her sacrifice, her love, was a small price to pay for their peace.

One night, after another ritualistic dose of her concoction, Catherine sat in the living room, watching her family slump quietly on the couch. James had his arm around Emily, who had fallen asleep with her head resting against his chest, while Nathan dozed in his lap. They all looked so peaceful, so serene, that Catherine couldn't help but smile. This was the life she had always dreamed of—perfect harmony, perfect peace. She was the one who had created this, who had molded them into the family she had always longed for.

The next morning, things went differently.

Catherine woke to find the house unusually still. The clock on the wall ticked loudly in the silence. She got up, feeling a sudden sense of unease, and went into the living room. James was still in his chair, but his body was cold. Emily lay next to him, unmoving. Nathan was curled up at their feet. A wave of panic hit her, and she rushed to check for signs of life, but there was nothing—no breath, no pulse.

Her mind raced, but the world around her seemed to slow. She stumbled back, her eyes wide with shock, and for a moment, she couldn't make sense of what she saw. The empty tea cup. The faint smell of something she couldn't quite place. It was then, when her hands trembled as she reached for her phone to call for help, that it hit her.

She had poisoned them all too much. In her desperate need to control, in her desire to make everything perfect, she had gone too far. They were gone. Her family, the perfect family, was gone.

Catherine collapsed to the floor, the weight of her actions crashing down on her all at once. She had taken them to a "better place," just as she had promised, but it wasn't the kind of peace she had imagined. It was a peace that had been bought with their lives, with her own selfish desire for control. She had sought perfection, but in the end, she had destroyed the very thing she loved most. The lesson was clear: love without boundaries, control without empathy, can only lead to destruction. And now, she was left with nothing but the hollow echo of her own twisted version of peace.

The Librarian's Recipe

Evelyn Whitmore was a quiet woman, and to most people, she was nothing more than a shadow in the corner of a large, musty library. She had been working there for nearly two decades, cataloging books, helping patrons, and keeping the library running smoothly. Her appearance was unremarkable—thin, with graying hair that she kept neatly pinned back, wearing glasses that made her seem even more distant and detached from the world. To the average person, she was invisible, just another fixture in the city.

But Evelyn's mind was sharp, and she carried secrets within her that no one would ever suspect. She had a deep knowledge of toxicology, learned from years of reading obscure texts in the back corners of the library, from devouring old medical journals, and from a quiet fascination with poisons. She had started young, hiding her curiosity behind a mask of innocence, but as she grew older, her obsession with the chemistry of death took root. She had learned how poisons worked, how to administer them, how to make them undetectable. To the outside world, she was just a librarian, but in her mind, she was something more—a judge, a punisher, a deliverer of justice.

It began with small acts. People who had wronged her—petty things, really. A rude patron who had complained about a late fine, a colleague who had taken credit for her work—nothing big, but the anger festered. She knew she couldn't lash out, not in a way that would raise suspicion, not in her line of work. But the power she could wield from the shadows, quietly tipping the balance of life and death, appealed to her more than she ever let on.

The first victim was Harold Thompson, a man who had made Evelyn's life difficult for years. Harold was a frequent visitor to the library, and despite his abrasive nature, he had the audacity to constantly criticize her for things she couldn't control—how the books were organized, how the computers worked, how long it took for the new titles to arrive. He had no respect for her, and his criticisms always struck deep into her pride. One evening, while Harold was checking out a pile of books, Evelyn slipped a small amount of ricin into his coffee—a substance she knew could easily go undetected in a hot beverage. She watched him sip it as she processed his check-out, a quiet smile on her lips. A few hours later, he was dead, the cause of his sudden illness officially listed as heart failure. No one suspected the librarian.

From there, Evelyn's confidence grew. She moved on to others who she believed deserved punishment—people who had wronged her, or simply those who lived in ways she thought were wasteful or ignorant. An arrogant professor who had treated her with condescension; a businessman who used his wealth to exploit the less fortunate; a corrupt politician she'd seen once on television—each one became part of her growing list. She researched their habits, their weaknesses, and she took great care in ensuring that her poison was undetected, that her methods were invisible. She crafted her poisons like a chef working on a fine recipe, each dose carefully calculated, each victim carefully chosen.

But what Evelyn did not anticipate was how much her own arrogance would grow with each success. She began to take pleasure in the control, in knowing that she could decide who lived and who died with nothing more than a subtle flick of her wrist, the quiet dropping of a powder into a glass or the mixing of a liquid into a meal. It became an addiction, the satisfaction of knowing she had caused the world to shift in her favor, without anyone ever knowing she was there.

As the years passed, Evelyn's actions became more brazen. She began to experiment with more complex poisons, more dangerous substances, each one more effective than the last. She would hide the poisons in places no one would think to look—within jars of jam, beneath layers of food, in bottles of wine she knew others would drink. Her obsession grew. She no longer limited herself to the judgment of the deserving few. Now, the list expanded—those she deemed unworthy, those she believed were failing society, or simply anyone she saw as a potential target. It didn't matter what their crime was. They had wronged the world in some way, and Evelyn had the right to balance the scales.

One morning, Evelyn noticed something that made her pause. There was a new detective in town, someone who had been investigating a string of strange deaths. Deaths that, in her mind, couldn't be connected. After all, she had been so careful, so precise. They were isolated incidents—accidents, natural causes. The thought that someone could see through her carefully constructed web was absurd. But the detective's presence made her uneasy.

Detective Laura Hayes had been quietly watching the town's rising number of unexplained deaths, noting a disturbing pattern. It was a slow burn, the kind of thing that couldn't be easily noticed until you stepped back far enough to see the larger picture. She hadn't made the connection yet, but something about the deaths felt wrong. They were too clean, too carefully planned. They didn't feel like random accidents. And so, she began to investigate.

Evelyn, however, wasn't worried at first. She was smart, and she had always stayed under the radar. No one suspected a librarian, no one suspected the quiet woman with the unassuming smile. But as the detective grew more persistent, as the investigation began to focus more on subtle poisons and undetectable substances, Evelyn felt her world start to crumble. She could feel the heat closing in, but there was no way to stop it. She had become too bold, too confident, and now there was a chance someone might uncover the truth.

In a final act of desperation, Evelyn tried to cover her tracks. She disposed of evidence, erased records, and took measures to make sure no one could connect her to the deaths. But in her frantic attempt to remain unseen, she had made a crucial mistake. She had underestimated the one thing she thought she had mastered—the ability to disappear.

Detective Hayes found the missing link: a small, overlooked detail in Evelyn's records. She found a pattern, not in the victims, but in the library's check-out system. Evelyn had been borrowing books on toxicology, books on poisons, over the years. She had been researching her own methods, her own techniques, and in the process, she had left a trail—a trail that led straight to her.

It was a simple thing, a small mistake, but it was enough. Evelyn's downfall wasn't the poisons she had so carefully crafted, nor the countless lives she had stolen. It was her overconfidence, the belief that she could outsmart everyone. She had failed to realize that, even in the quietest corners of the world, there is always someone watching, always someone who can see through the carefully constructed facades.

As Evelyn was arrested, the twisted irony of it all struck her. She had spent years meticulously erasing every trace of herself, but in the end, she was undone by her own arrogance. And as Detective Hayes prepared to take her into custody, Evelyn realized that there had been one thing she hadn't accounted for—the lesson of being too invisible for too long.

The Last Job

Rachel hadn't always been the woman she was now. In another life, she had been a daughter, a sister, someone who laughed freely and dreamed of a future beyond the shadows. But those dreams had long since evaporated, buried beneath years of violence, blood, and the hollow promises made to herself that she could walk away from it all. Once, Rachel had been just another assassin, a shadow in the underworld, taking jobs for the right price. But over time, the line between professional and personal had blurred.

Her reputation as one of the best in the business had been built on precision, coldness, and a complete lack of emotional attachment. For years, she had worked for people who needed someone eliminated, targets that didn't matter beyond the money they could pay. She had always done what was asked, never questioning, never second-guessing. She was good at it—too good.

But when her mother had died, a sudden, brutal death caused by a car accident that never quite sat right with her, everything changed. No one had ever suspected foul play. The accident had been deemed just that—an accident. But Rachel knew better. She knew someone had orchestrated it. Someone had planned her mother's death, and she was left with the crushing reality that she could do nothing to bring her back. Grief turned to anger, and anger became a craving for revenge.

It started small. She wasn't sure who to target first, but she knew that whoever had taken her mother's life would pay. Rachel began her own investigation. Her past connections helped, and after months of digging, she found her first suspect: A crooked businessman, Charles Davenport, a man with deep ties to the underground world. He had been the one to pull the strings, the one who had made the call, ensuring her mother's death was made to look like an accident.

The plan was simple: infiltrate his life, learn his habits, and make him disappear. He was just another target, but Rachel's motives were personal this time. When she finally had him alone in a secluded part of the city, her heart didn't race like it used to when she had killed for pay. This was different. This was catharsis. She shot him in the head, her mind clear, her movements practiced. But as she watched his body hit the ground, a strange sense of satisfaction washed over her, a sense of completion. His death was the start of a new chapter—one where she wouldn't take orders anymore. Now, she was the one in control.

Rachel quickly realized that she could not stop at just Charles Davenport. Her need for vengeance was insatiable, and she began hunting down others she believed were responsible for her mother's death. Some were directly involved, others had only been peripheral, but they were all connected to the same corrupt network. She killed without remorse, moving through the world with the precision of a machine. Each death felt like a small step toward reclaiming her lost humanity, a small piece of justice restored.

But as the bodies piled up, something darker began to emerge. The lines between her work as an assassin and her thirst for revenge blurred further. She was no longer just eliminating people who had crossed her. She started targeting anyone who had wronged her in any way—slights from her past, old grudges that had been forgotten by everyone except her. It didn't matter whether they had been directly involved in her mother's death; Rachel didn't care anymore. The people she killed no longer had to be connected to her mother's accident. They just had to have wronged her in some way, whether it was personal, financial, or even just a fleeting insult.

The darker Rachel became, the harder it was to keep her emotions in check. She had crossed a line that she couldn't return from. At first, she told herself it was just business, that this was what she had always done. But the truth was, each death had become more personal. The faces of those she killed began to blur with the faces of those she had lost. Every time she took another life, it was like scratching an itch that could never be fully scratched.

It was the night she targeted her old mentor, Simon Adler, that everything truly unraveled. Simon had taught her everything she knew about the business—how to kill, how to disappear, how to keep a low profile. He had been like a father to her, someone she trusted implicitly. But after her mother's death, when she tried to ask him for help, Simon had turned his back on her. He told her that it was just business, that everyone had to die eventually, and that revenge wouldn't bring her mother back.

It had crushed her. Simon's cold, pragmatic response had sent her spiraling. In that moment, she had realized that he, too, was part of the system she had come to despise. He wasn't just a mentor—he was a part of the machine that had killed her mother, a piece of the puzzle that she had to destroy.

Simon didn't see it coming. Rachel made her way to his home, moving quietly through the shadows, as she always did. She had learned everything about him, from his habits to his weaknesses, over the years. But when she entered his house and saw him sitting there, waiting for her, something inside her faltered. He had known she was coming. He had known she would eventually come for him.

"Is this what you wanted?" Simon asked, his voice calm, almost resigned.

Rachel hesitated for a moment, the gun still in her hand. "You betrayed me," she whispered, her voice trembling.

Simon's expression softened, but there was no fear in his eyes. He had seen too much to fear death anymore. "You're not the person you think you are, Rachel. You're not the victim. You're the one becoming the monster."

But it was too late. With a swift motion, she pulled the trigger, and Simon fell to the floor, his blood mixing with the shadows. As she stood over his body, Rachel felt a strange emptiness settle in her chest. She had killed him. But she had also killed the last part of herself that had still believed she was doing something noble. She was no longer the woman she had been. She had become something darker, something irreversible.

As the night faded into morning, Rachel sat in the silence of Simon's house, surrounded by death. She had completed her vengeance, but at what cost? She had destroyed the one person who had ever cared for her, the one person who had always guided her. She had blurred the lines between business and personal, and now, she was left with nothing but the consequences of her actions.

In that moment, Rachel realized that there was no redemption for her. The vengeance she had sought had only deepened her darkness. What had begun as a mission for justice had turned into something far worse—a cycle of violence that would never end. She had become the very thing she had once hunted, and now, there was no escape from the monster she had become.

This content may violate our usage policies[1].

Did we get it wrong? Please tell us by giving this response a thumbs down.

---

1.   https://openai.com/policies/usage-policies

The Golden Trap

Linda Hamilton had long since mastered the art of allure. In her late thirties, she was a woman who exuded wealth, power, and a sense of grace that made younger men gravitate toward her. She was the embodiment of confidence, a woman who knew what she wanted and had the means to get it. Her large, pristine home in the heart of the city was a testament to her success, a world of luxury that no one could penetrate unless she allowed it. But Linda had a secret, one that she had carefully cultivated over the years—a secret that made her the queen of an unspoken game.

Linda was a *sugar mama*, but not in the way most would think. She didn't just offer lavish gifts or a luxurious lifestyle. She offered a twisted kind of control—an irresistible bait for those desperate enough to fall into her trap. Young men, most of them in their early twenties, were drawn to her wealth, her maturity, and the illusion of stability she projected. To them, she was a goddess, a fairy tale wrapped in designer clothes and a promising future. And to Linda, they were nothing more than pawns in a sick game that played out again and again.

Her approach was always the same. She would find them—usually through dating apps, where men posted photos of their muscles and smiles, searching for someone who could make their dreams come true. Linda would take her time, carefully studying each one, making sure they fit her needs: charming enough to seduce her, vulnerable enough to need her, and naïve enough to think they had the upper hand. She would draw them in with promises of excitement and luxury, offering them the life they never thought possible. In return, they would provide her with companionship, a temporary feeling of youth, and most importantly, access to the money she desired.

It had always worked—*always*—but it wasn't just about the money. Linda wasn't a desperate woman looking for love or affection. She didn't need a relationship to feel whole. What Linda craved, what she needed, was the power. The power to control someone's life, to watch them crumble as they realized they had nothing left to give, nothing but themselves. And when they were drained, when they had nothing else to offer her, Linda would dispose of them. Slowly, methodically, without a hint of regret.

Tonight was no different. She had met Mark a few months ago, a young man who was everything she had ever wanted in a plaything—handsome, eager to please, and utterly dependent on her for the lavish lifestyle he had never known. Linda had been generous, taking him on trips, buying him expensive clothes, giving him more attention than anyone had ever given him before. Mark worshipped her, not realizing that he was being bled dry, both emotionally and financially. He had no idea that his usefulness had an expiration date.

Linda had carefully orchestrated the end, just as she always did. She had made sure Mark had racked up credit card bills he could never pay, bought extravagant gifts that he thought were signs of her affection. She knew exactly what to do to make him feel like he was the center of her world. She knew how to make him believe that his needs, his desires, were the only things that mattered.

Now, as she sat across from him at the dinner table, watching him devour the expensive meal she had prepared, Linda felt a twisted satisfaction. Mark had no idea that tonight would be the last time he would sit at her table. He smiled at her, his eyes wide with adoration, completely unaware of the plans she had for him.

"Linda, you really are amazing," Mark said, his voice sincere. "I've never felt like this before. I don't know how I got so lucky."

Linda smiled back, the charm never leaving her face. "You're welcome, Mark. I'm glad you're happy." She paused, letting the moment hang in the air. "But sometimes, happiness comes at a cost."

Mark looked confused, his smile faltering slightly. "What do you mean?"

Linda's gaze hardened, though she kept her voice steady. "Nothing is ever free, Mark. Not in this world."

She stood up, walking to the kitchen counter where she had placed the drink. She had been careful about the dose, just as she always was—enough to make him slip into unconsciousness, but not enough for anyone to notice. She poured it into his glass, watching the color change ever so slightly, just enough to be undetectable to him. When she returned, she handed it to him with a smile.

"Drink up, darling. You've earned it."

Mark took the glass without hesitation, raising it to her in a gesture of gratitude. "To us," he said, and he drank deeply.

Linda watched as his face slowly began to lose its color, his eyes becoming heavy. He didn't suspect a thing. He was too blinded by his own desires, too consumed by the lavish lifestyle she had promised him. But Linda wasn't concerned about the money or the material things anymore. She had long since grown bored of the games. It wasn't about the riches or the excitement. It was about the end. The final moment when she could see the last traces of their hope and dreams fade away.

Mark slumped in his chair, his head lolling to the side. He was out, his body completely at her mercy.

Linda stood over him, her fingers lightly tracing the edge of the glass. She had already disposed of the last few who had overstayed their welcome, who had outlived their usefulness. But as she looked down at Mark's lifeless body, something unexpected flickered in her heart—a brief, fleeting moment of doubt.

She had done this so many times before, but this time, it felt different. She had always seen them as tools, objects to be used, discarded when they no longer served their purpose. But as she stood there, contemplating the finality of it, she realized something about herself—something dark and unsettling.

She didn't just kill them because they had drained her. She killed them because she was terrified of being drained herself. Terrified of needing someone, terrified of someone needing her in return. It wasn't about power or control, it was about fear. Fear of being vulnerable. Fear of being left empty. She had convinced herself she was a queen, ruling over her kingdom of broken men, but in the end, she had become just as hollow as they had.

As the truth settled over her, Linda realized that the moment of power she had craved had always been fleeting. She had drained Mark to fill the emptiness, but there would always be another, and another, until there was no one left to deceive.

And in the silence that followed, Linda understood the real cost of her games. It wasn't just the men she had killed, but the woman she had become—the monster hiding behind the mask of generosity. The trap she had set for them was the same trap she had set for herself.

The Final Autopsy

Dr. Caroline Hayes was respected. No one doubted her abilities. As the lead medical examiner in a mid-sized city, she was known for her precision, her cold professionalism, and her unflinching ability to uncover the truth behind each body she examined. She had built her career on this reputation—cold, calculated, an expert in determining causes of death with meticulous care. But there was more to Caroline than anyone realized, more than anyone could have guessed. She was a woman with a dark secret, one that began long before she had entered the world of forensic pathology.

Caroline had always been fascinated by death, by the way it left its mark on the human body. As a child, she would bury small animals in her backyard, study them from the moment they passed to understand their final moments. This curiosity had led her to study medicine, eventually specializing in forensic pathology. It was her calling, a way for her to satisfy that dark thirst inside her. But over the years, as she saw death after death, she began to feel something else—something more sinister. She wanted to *control* death, to understand it not just as an observer, but as a participant.

The idea first crossed her mind during a routine autopsy. A young man had been brought in, a victim of what appeared to be a car accident. Caroline performed the usual examination, determined that the cause of death was blunt force trauma, and signed the report. But as she examined his body, something about him caught her attention. He was so young, so full of life, and yet so helpless under the precision of her scalpel. She could almost feel his last moments in the quiet hum of her tools. And then, as if by accident, she pricked her finger on a needle while extracting a sample. The blood was warm. She froze. That fleeting moment, that connection, set something off in her.

The next few months passed in a haze, until she began noticing patterns in the cases she examined. Suicides, overdoses, accidents—each case she looked at seemed a little too convenient, a little too perfect. No one questioned the deaths. No one suspected foul play. It was the perfect cover for her growing need. So, she began to experiment. She carefully selected her victims—those who didn't matter, those who no one would miss. She would inject them with an overdose of insulin or a lethal dose of a commonly prescribed drug, carefully adjusting the dose until it was just enough to kill them slowly.

Then, as the victim died, Caroline would document the cause of death as a natural one, sometimes adding the faintest traces of evidence to make it seem as though the person had simply slipped away, had faded into nothingness. Afterward, she would conduct the autopsy herself, playing the role of the detached investigator. She took great care in framing the deaths as "accidental" or "natural causes," covering her tracks by altering small details. She made sure no one suspected her, and no one ever did. She was the perfect medical examiner—the expert on death, the one person everyone trusted.

Caroline felt a sense of power she had never known. She had complete control over life and death, and no one suspected a thing. She felt her emotions slipping away as her actions became more and more deliberate, more calculated. She was doing a service, she convinced herself. Those people she killed—her "subjects" as she called them—had been nothing but burdens on the world. Their deaths were a mercy, a release from their suffering, even if they had never asked for it. It wasn't about the victims. It was about Caroline. It was about the control she had over them, the power to make life disappear with a single action.

But as the number of deaths rose, so did her confidence. She began to take greater risks, targeting people who were closer to the system—someone who worked in the office across from hers, a colleague she had grown to despise for his smug attitude. She injected him with a lethal dose of a fast-acting drug, making sure it was undetectable. The next day, she performed the autopsy, documenting the cause of death as a heart attack. He was found hours later, his body still warm from the drug's effects. No one questioned it. No one suspected foul play. Caroline was invincible.

But as she took more lives, something began to change inside her. The thrill of controlling death had dulled. The bodies on her table became increasingly impersonal, their stories less significant. She no longer felt the rush she had once felt. Something was missing. She needed more.

Then, one day, a case came in that would change everything. A woman had been found dead in her home, the victim of an apparent overdose. The woman had been a friend of Caroline's, someone she had known for years. Caroline felt a pang of regret when she saw her friend's name in the case file. She had been close to her once, but their friendship had fallen apart when the woman had made a series of bad decisions, each one more reckless than the last. Caroline had tried to warn her, tried to offer help, but her friend had turned away, choosing instead to follow a dangerous path.

Caroline saw it as a kind of justice—her friend had been so foolish, so careless with her life, and now, she would be gone. This time, Caroline didn't need to set it up. Her friend's death would be the perfect opportunity to test her limits, to see how far she could go without being caught. She told herself it was fate. The overdose would be ruled as an accident, a tragic consequence of her friend's own choices.

As Caroline conducted the autopsy, she felt the familiar thrill course through her veins. She found the traces of the drug, the ones she had carefully administered, and noted the cause of death in her report. But then something unexpected happened. As she examined her friend's body, she realized that something was wrong. The woman's face looked familiar in a way that unsettled her. The features were slightly altered, the expressions too much like her own.

In that moment, Caroline understood. She had done it. She had killed her own reflection. She had created her own monster. Her friend was a mirror of everything she had become, and by erasing her, she had erased the last piece of herself that was still human. She had been so focused on her own power, on her ability to control death, that she hadn't seen the toll it had taken on her soul.

Her hand shook as she wrote the cause of death, but it was too late. She had crossed the line, and now, there was no going back. The woman she had killed was not just a victim—she was Caroline's final undoing.

As the door to the examination room closed behind her, Caroline realized the truth too late. In the pursuit of power over life and death, she had destroyed her own.

The Hollow Rite

Marissa Kingsley was a woman of presence, and when she walked into a room, you noticed. It wasn't just her physical appearance—though she was striking in a way that commanded attention—but the air around her, a calm authority that seemed to settle over others like a thick fog. She was known in her community as a spiritual healer, a woman who could clear the body and soul of dark energy with nothing more than her words and touch. Her small, modest practice was nestled in a quiet corner of town, a place where the weary came for solace, the broken came for hope, and the desperate came for answers. It was the kind of place where miracles were whispered about, and where no one asked too many questions.

Marissa had built her reputation on the stories of her successes. She claimed she had been trained by a long line of spiritual healers, anointed to carry out the sacred work of ridding people of the demons that plagued their minds, their bodies, and their souls. She conducted her exorcisms with an intensity that seemed almost divine. And though there was a touch of theater to her performances—an eerie chant here, a moment of silence there—no one doubted that she had something special, something that set her apart from other practitioners. It wasn't magic. It wasn't even faith, really. What made Marissa different was her ability to get inside her patients' heads, to feed on their vulnerabilities, to play on their deepest fears, and in doing so, convince them they were truly possessed.

The truth was, Marissa had no special gifts. She had no divine connection, no ancient wisdom passed down through generations. She had simply learned the art of manipulation. She understood the human mind better than anyone. She knew how to push the right buttons, to plant the seed of doubt, to make someone question their own sanity. All she needed was a broken soul, and Marissa knew how to find them. They were the lost, the lonely, the ones who had nowhere else to turn.

She would listen patiently to their stories, their tales of inner torment, their struggle to connect with anything beyond their own pain. And she would offer them salvation. At least, that's what they thought.

Her most recent client, Sarah, was just the kind of person Marissa thrived on. Sarah had lost her job, had gone through a divorce, and her health had started to fail. She was at rock bottom, and she believed—no, *desperately wanted to believe*—that there was something wrong with her, something inside her that was beyond her control. She had become convinced that evil spirits were responsible for all her misfortunes. The more Marissa listened, the more she saw the opportunity.

The first time Sarah came to her, Marissa put on her softest, most compassionate smile. "You're not alone," she told Sarah. "You are simply carrying the weight of things that were never yours to bear." She gently took Sarah's hands in hers, looking into her eyes as if she could see her very soul. "But I can help you release it, if you trust me."

Sarah nodded, her eyes filled with both fear and hope. "I need to be free of this... this darkness inside me," she whispered.

The exorcism was set. Marissa promised Sarah that she would guide her through the process, that together they would expel the demons that were preventing her from living a peaceful life. It was all part of the plan, Marissa's carefully orchestrated charade. The ritual began with a chant, soft and melodic at first, slowly increasing in intensity. Marissa led Sarah through deep breathing exercises, asking her to close her eyes and concentrate on the sensation of the air filling her lungs, the power she would feel once the demons had been expelled. Sarah's face twisted in concentration, her fingers gripping the armrests as Marissa's voice grew more commanding.

At first, Sarah resisted. There were moments when Marissa could see the skepticism flicker in her eyes, the doubt creeping in as she wondered if this was really working, if she was just playing into some sort of charlatan's game. But then Marissa would say something—something about Sarah's past, about the guilt she carried, the regret she felt over her failed marriage—and Sarah would break. Her body would shake, her breathing would quicken, and she would give in to the catharsis that Marissa expertly guided her through. It was always the same: the tears, the sobs, the violent thrashing, as if she was truly being freed from something evil. And when it was over, Sarah would collapse in a heap, drained but relieved, convinced she was no longer possessed.

But Marissa knew better. She knew that nothing had changed. Sarah's pain had not been exorcised; it had simply been redirected. Marissa had given her no real answers, no real healing—only the illusion of release. And Sarah, in her fragile state, clung to that illusion, willing to pay whatever it took for a little more peace, a little more comfort. And so, Marissa took advantage of that. She took Sarah's money, smiled sweetly, and promised to continue working with her, each exorcism a little more intense, a little more draining than the last, until Sarah was so dependent on her that she no longer questioned the cost of the treatments.

Weeks went by, and Sarah's condition worsened. Her health deteriorated, her strength sapped by the rituals, and yet she never once thought to ask if Marissa's methods were truly helping. She had been told that it was all part of the process, that healing required sacrifice, and that she needed to give more of herself to become truly free. Marissa's hold on her grew stronger with each passing day.

Then, one night, Sarah came to Marissa's office looking more desperate than ever. "I feel it again," she said, trembling. "It's inside me. I can't breathe. It's suffocating me." Her eyes were wide with fear. "Please, you have to help me."

Marissa's heart beat faster—not out of concern, but out of excitement. This was the moment she had been waiting for. This was the time to finish what she had started.

"I know exactly what you need," Marissa said, her voice a soothing whisper. She took Sarah's hand and led her to the table where the last ritual would take place. This time, the poison she had slipped into Sarah's water would be the final part of the ritual. As Sarah lay there, her breath slow and labored, Marissa whispered in her ear, "This will be the last time, Sarah. You'll finally be free."

And with that, Sarah's body went limp, her struggles ceasing as she fell into the deepest sleep, the final death brought on by the very healer she trusted. Marissa stood over her, her face expressionless, as she admired the perfect outcome of her manipulation. She had done it—Sarah was gone, and Marissa had claimed victory once more.

But as Marissa wiped her hands clean, a thought lingered in her mind. She had preyed on Sarah's vulnerability, convincing her she needed something that was never real. In the end, it wasn't the demons that had killed Sarah. It was her own desperate need to believe in the lie. And for the first time, Marissa felt the sharp sting of doubt in the pit of her stomach. Had Sarah truly been possessed by something dark, or had it just been the darkness of her own fear?

The Open House

Clara Matthews was the type of woman who could sell anything. She had spent over a decade in real estate, building a reputation for herself that was as immaculate as the pristine homes she represented. Her clients adored her professionalism, her sharp attention to detail, and the way she could seamlessly guide them through the process of purchasing a new home. She was good at her job, perhaps even too good. But her success had its cost.

Beneath her polished exterior, Clara was constantly battling feelings of inadequacy. Despite her thriving career, her elegant wardrobe, and the envy of her peers, she couldn't escape the gnawing sensation that she was never enough. There were always those who made her feel inferior—buyers who would glance at her, their eyes briefly flicking to her attire, then dismiss her with a polite but cold smile. They were rich, confident, and often condescending, as if her role as a real estate agent somehow made her less than them. In those moments, Clara would feel herself shrink inside, her heart sinking, the invisible walls around her closing in.

The first one was an accident. Or at least, that's how Clara justified it to herself. Derek Grant was one of those buyers. He had come to her with an air of superiority, scanning each house with a critical eye, making judgmental comments about the homes she showed him. It wasn't the houses he disliked—it was her. She could see it in the way his lips curled up slightly, as though he couldn't fathom why someone like him would need to be shown these "modest" properties. He didn't respect her. He didn't respect anyone who wasn't on his level. His words were always polished, polite even, but the underlying disdain was unmistakable. Clara's patience wore thin the longer she worked with him.

One rainy afternoon, Derek had insisted on seeing a mansion on the outskirts of town. The property had been on the market for months, and despite its size and opulence, it hadn't sold. Clara had made the mistake of telling him that it was priced higher than some of the other homes in the area, and Derek had made a dismissive comment about the asking price, implying that it was beneath him to even consider such a purchase. His arrogance had stung. That was when the thought had first crossed Clara's mind—if she could just make him feel the way he made her feel. Just for a moment.

They had taken a private tour of the house, Derek's voice echoing off the grand walls as he critiqued everything. He was walking ahead of her, his back turned as he examined the grand staircase. Clara stepped lightly behind him, her fingers brushing against the balustrade. The staircase was old, the banister worn with age. A small part of her wondered if the old wood was sturdy enough to hold his weight. She hadn't expected him to turn, but when he did, his foot slipped—his body twisting awkwardly as he lost balance. The fall was slow, almost cinematic in its unfolding. Derek's body hit the floor with a sickening thud, his neck snapping violently as his skull struck the hardwood.

For a moment, Clara froze. The silence in the house was deafening. And then she heard the rush of her own breath, the racing of her pulse. She stood over Derek's lifeless body, the absurdity of what had just happened washing over her. She didn't scream. She didn't panic. Instead, she moved swiftly, almost methodically. She checked the body—he was dead, his neck broken in a way that made it impossible for anyone to argue otherwise.

Clara made sure to stage the scene carefully. She positioned his body so it looked like he had tripped on the top step, falling forward in the most tragic of accidents. She rearranged a few items around the room to make it look like he had been exploring on his own when it happened. No one would question it. It would look like an unfortunate mishap. She was confident. She had been in the business of selling stories for years. She could sell this.

The police arrived hours later, and as Clara watched them from the corner of the room, she felt the heavy weight of her own calmness. They investigated, questioned her, but found nothing suspicious. Clara was the grieving agent, the woman who had witnessed the tragedy unfold. She could feel herself slipping into the role she had rehearsed over and over in her head. And when they left, Derek's body was taken away, and the mansion was marked for sale once more.

But Clara didn't stop there. As the days went by, she found herself planning more carefully, more deliberately. She targeted men like Derek—the ones who had made her feel small, the ones who had dismissed her presence as nothing more than a vehicle for their own desires. She lured them in with promises of the perfect property, their egos fed with talk of exclusivity and luxury. Each man was a little different, but the outcome was always the same. She would offer them a private tour of a grand estate, a house that had yet to sell, the kind of property that required a certain kind of buyer. And when they were alone, she would strike—subtly, quietly, watching them fall from grace, their lives extinguished with a coldness she had come to relish.

Each death was flawless. The men were all wealthy, powerful, men who could afford to be careless, who thought the world owed them something. Clara knew how to manipulate them, how to make them feel invincible, just long enough to slip them into a place where they felt they were in control. And when their grip on that control faltered—when they tripped or slipped, falling victim to their own hubris—Clara would be there, ready to carry out her plan. Each time, she made sure to stage the deaths carefully, ensuring no one suspected foul play. She had become an expert in orchestrating their final moments.

It wasn't until the last one that she felt the slightest twinge of hesitation. The man's name was Michael Travers—a real estate mogul with an inflated sense of self-importance. He had been dismissive of her for weeks, always treating her as nothing more than an accessory to his ambition. Their final meeting had been at a luxurious property she had selected specifically for him, one that had been on the market for months and yet remained unsold. She had set everything up, prepared everything just as she had done before.

But as Michael leaned in to inspect the staircase, the thought crossed her mind: *What if this wasn't enough? What if she had become just like them—the ones who had seen her as a means to an end?*

She stepped behind him, as she always did, but this time, as his body began to fall, something in her snapped. She watched him hit the floor, the same sickening sound echoing through the house. And in that moment, she felt nothing. No triumph. No relief. Only emptiness. She had become the very thing she despised—cold, calculating, a woman who had played her own game and had no one left to turn to.

Clara didn't bother with the usual staging. Instead, she left him where he had fallen, abandoned by the very thing that had once given her power—her own sense of control. The truth had sunk in too deep. She had killed for revenge, for self-preservation, but in the end, it wasn't the men who had used her who were the problem. It was her own inability to stop, to ever feel enough.

The Benevolent Hand

Martha Jennings was a woman admired by many. She ran *Hope Haven*, a well-known foster care agency that had been the recipient of numerous accolades and public recognition. She had dedicated her life to caring for children who had been abandoned, neglected, or abused. Her agency, nestled in a quiet corner of the city, housed dozens of children, each with their own tragic story. Martha was the epitome of kindness, the face of compassion. She was the one the community turned to when they needed someone to make a difference in the lives of vulnerable children. She had built *Hope Haven* from the ground up, pouring every ounce of her energy into making it a safe haven for those who had no one else to turn to.

But beneath her perfectly manicured façade, Martha harbored a darkness—an insatiable hunger that she had learned to conceal over the years. Her motivations for running the agency weren't as pure as the world thought. She didn't just want to help the children. She wanted control over them. She craved the power of life and death, the ability to shape their fates in her hands.

It began with small acts of cruelty. A child who needed extra care, a special one that would require more attention than the others, would be chosen. They were the ones who seemed the most fragile, the ones who couldn't protect themselves, the ones no one would miss if they disappeared. It wasn't always obvious at first. A little more medication here, a little less food there. Small things, things that could be brushed off as part of the natural ebb and flow of foster care. She would ensure they received the necessary treatment, but sometimes, the treatment would go awry. And the best part was, no one would question her. She was the caregiver, the one with the answers, the one who could be trusted to make the tough decisions.

One child, in particular, caught her eye. His name was Joshua. He was seven years old, with big brown eyes that looked far too old for his age. He had been taken from a broken home, his mother lost in a battle with addiction, his father long gone. When he arrived at *Hope Haven*, he was shy, withdrawn, but Martha knew what she could do. He would be the perfect subject. He was small, easy to manipulate, and no one would notice if something happened to him. She convinced herself that he needed her more than the others—he needed special care, a nurturing touch that only she could give.

At first, she kept her distance, observing him, watching him like a hawk. But soon, she began to push the boundaries. She would feed him smaller portions of food, just enough to make him weak, to drain his energy, while the others ate heartily. He started to look more frail, his skin pale and sickly. When the other children noticed, Martha would tell them that Joshua was just a little more sensitive, that he needed extra rest. The excuses came naturally. No one questioned her. She was the expert, after all.

But as time went on, her manipulations became more deliberate. She would introduce him to medications that weren't on the approved list, things she knew could cause him to become more subdued, more malleable. She would make sure he was always in the right place at the right time—where she could control him without interference. His energy began to wane, and his eyes lost that last bit of life they had once held. Joshua was fading, but no one knew. They trusted Martha. She had a way of making everyone believe that she was the answer. She was the good one, the one who could make everything better. She could fix anything.

It was the night of the incident that everything came to a head. Joshua had been particularly lethargic that day, and Martha had decided it was time to put her plan into motion. She had carefully prepared a dose of sedatives, just enough to knock him out completely.

She told herself it would be quick, that it would just put him to sleep. She told herself she was doing the right thing—this was the only way to end his suffering, the only way to give him peace.

Martha slipped into his room after the others had gone to bed, her heart pounding in anticipation. She gently shook Joshua awake, whispering comforting words in his ear as she slipped the drug into his drink. He drank it without question, trusting her completely. It wasn't long before his body went limp, his breath shallow. He was under. She stood over him, her breath steady, her hands cold. She watched him for a few moments, making sure the drug had taken effect. But something about his stillness, his quiet surrender, disturbed her.

She had done this many times before—only now, something didn't feel right. She was supposed to feel relief, satisfaction that she had made the right choice. But instead, there was a creeping sense of emptiness, a growing realization that perhaps this was not what she had thought it would be. Joshua's life had been in her hands, and she had chosen to snuff it out. There was no comfort, no peace. There was only an absence, a void where his life should have been.

Martha sat by his bed, watching him sleep, her mind racing. The sound of the house settling, the hum of the refrigerator in the kitchen, the soft creak of the floorboards—everything seemed so distant. She had taken a life, but in doing so, she had revealed a truth she couldn't ignore: there was no power in death, only emptiness. She had created her own illusion of control, convincing herself that she could fix these children, mold them into what she needed them to be. But in the end, she had only destroyed them. She had been the one who needed saving.

As the hours passed, Martha stayed at Joshua's side, until a quiet knock on the door broke her reverie. It was another foster parent, one of the others who occasionally worked with her. They had come to check in on Joshua after hearing reports of his condition. Martha quickly hid the evidence, rearranging her composure. She greeted the worker with a smile, her hands still trembling but perfectly poised.

The next morning, when Joshua's body was discovered, it was ruled an accident. The medical examiner found no clear signs of foul play. It was attributed to a series of unfortunate events—his fragile health, the exhaustion that had drained him, the mix of medications that had been accidentally administered. No one questioned it. No one ever suspected Martha.

But deep down, Martha knew the truth. And as she continued her work at *Hope Haven*, the emptiness inside her grew. She had learned the hard way that controlling others, manipulating their lives for her own twisted sense of power, would never satisfy her. She had taken away what she could never replace.

The Long Haul

Charlotte was a woman of few words. She didn't need to speak much to make her presence known. The roar of her truck engine was enough to announce her arrival, the sound of a beast that could travel across the country, covering hundreds of miles without stopping. She had spent years behind the wheel, hauling loads from coast to coast, living on the road, away from the noise of the world she had left behind. Most people never took a second glance at truck drivers—they were simply part of the background, the endless stream of vehicles moving across the highway. But Charlotte had learned to love the anonymity, the endless horizon that stretched out in front of her.

It wasn't the long hours or the solitude that kept her on the road—it was the opportunity. You see, Charlotte had a dark secret. Her job wasn't just a means to an end, it wasn't just about hauling freight. She had learned to use her truck as a vehicle for something far darker. The road, with its isolated stretches and quiet towns, was her hunting ground. And hitchhikers, travelers, the lost souls who crossed her path—well, they were just the kind of prey she had been waiting for.

She had no particular type—no specific profile of who she chose—but she had learned to spot them, those who seemed to trust too easily, those whose eyes didn't reflect the kind of wariness that came with being on the road. There were always the ones who needed help, the ones who smiled as they climbed into the passenger seat, oblivious to the danger that sat beside them. Charlotte never rushed. She never panicked. Her victims, always strangers, always seemed to vanish without a trace. A quick stop at a rest area, a quiet pull over to the side of the road, and that was the last anyone would see of them.

She didn't need to keep trophies. The thrill wasn't in keeping mementos—it was in the act itself, in the quiet violence of it all. The way their faces changed when they realized they weren't just on a ride to nowhere, but to their deaths. It wasn't always easy—sometimes it took days for the bodies to be found—but Charlotte always made sure the deaths seemed like accidents, tragedies that couldn't be explained.

One summer evening, Charlotte found herself in a small town in Wyoming. She had just dropped off a load of supplies at a warehouse and had a few hours to kill before her next pick-up. The sun was setting, casting long shadows across the empty highway. She parked her truck by the diner, eyes scanning the parking lot. That's when she saw him—Adam, a young man with a backpack slung over his shoulder, standing at the side of the road with his thumb outstretched, hopeful eyes scanning the horizon.

He was exactly the type Charlotte was looking for—young, naive, and looking for someone to trust. The world seemed to weigh on him, just enough to make him willing to take a chance. She knew it wouldn't take much. She slowed the truck down as she approached, rolling down the passenger window.

"Need a ride?" she asked, her voice soft, smooth.

Adam smiled, a weary grin that spoke of long days and lonely nights on the road. "Yeah, thanks," he said, climbing into the cab without a second thought.

Charlotte could almost taste the anticipation in the air as they drove out of the town. The hum of the truck's engine was the only sound between them, the road stretching endlessly ahead. She kept her eyes on the road, but her thoughts were elsewhere. She had already decided what would happen next.

"So, where you headed?" she asked, breaking the silence.

"California," Adam replied, leaning back in his seat, still looking out the window. "I'm just trying to get there, you know? Hoping to find something better. A job. Something..."

"Mm," Charlotte nodded, pretending to listen. "I get that. It's tough out here. People are always running from something, aren't they?"

Adam didn't respond, just nodded, his gaze turning inward. She could see the weariness in him, the uncertainty. It was perfect. He wasn't looking for danger. He wasn't thinking about the threat that sat beside him, driving him into the vast, dark world beyond the town.

The highway grew quieter as they passed through a stretch of land with little more than the occasional sign and a few scattered buildings. Charlotte's hand drifted down to the space beneath the seat, where she kept her tools—a simple thing, easy to reach. Adam was talking again, his voice fading into the background as her mind focused. He was still oblivious.

It wasn't until they were deep in the quiet stretch of road, with no houses in sight and the sky darkening above them, that Charlotte made her move. She pulled off the road, parking in a small, isolated spot surrounded by trees. Adam barely had time to register her sudden stop before she turned to him with a smile, the kind she had practiced a thousand times.

"Let's get you settled in for the night, alright?" she said.

Adam blinked, his confusion shifting into a smile of his own. "What do you mean?"

Charlotte's smile didn't waver. "Just a little detour. Trust me."

Before Adam could react, she was on him—quick, efficient. The knife she had taken from the small compartment beneath her seat found its mark in his side before he even realized what was happening. His breath caught in his throat, his eyes wide with shock as she twisted the blade. Charlotte didn't hesitate; she didn't need to. She had done this before, many times. Her mind was cold, her movements practiced.

The world outside seemed to fade as she focused on the task at hand. His struggling was brief, and his life slipped away like sand through her fingers. She made sure to wipe the blood away, to clean up the mess, making sure there was no trace left of Adam. When she finished, she set the truck back in motion, driving on without a second thought. He wouldn't be missed. He was just another ghost in the wind, another lost soul swallowed by the road.

It wasn't until much later that Charlotte realized the twist of fate that had followed her through all her years on the road. She had always chosen the ones who seemed vulnerable, the ones who couldn't see the danger right in front of them. And she had taken so much from them—their lives, their futures, their stories.

But she hadn't considered how much *she* had lost, how much of herself had slipped away, until she glanced into the rearview mirror that night. There, in the fading light, she saw a figure standing by the side of the road—another traveler, another soul walking through the darkness.

For the first time, Charlotte didn't slow down. She didn't need to. She had already become the thing she had always feared: a lost traveler, forever on the road, forever haunted by the ghosts she had left behind. The road that had given her power had also taken it all.

The Golden Cage

Emma had always been a beauty. She had the kind of face that stopped traffic—delicate features, wide eyes, soft lips. The kind of beauty that made men forget their manners and their morals. It was a gift she had learned to wield with precision, like a weapon crafted just for her. She knew exactly how to smile, how to bat her lashes, how to speak in just the right way to make a man feel like the most important person in the world. Her charm was effortless, but beneath that exterior, there was a coldness, an emptiness that Emma had learned to mask with every breath.

Emma was eighteen the first time she married. It wasn't love—it never was. It was a means to an end. Gregory was an older man, in his early fifties, and his wealth had made him an irresistible target. He had built a fortune in real estate and lived in a sprawling estate on the edge of town. He was lonely, desperate for affection, and Emma knew how to give him exactly what he wanted. She played the role of the sweet, innocent young woman who looked up to him with adoration, who seemed to cherish every word he spoke. But in truth, Emma had no interest in Gregory. She wanted his money. And she knew that with his heart in her hands, she could get it.

The marriage started out like all the others would—perfect, idyllic even. Gregory was wrapped around her finger, his wealth and influence now at her disposal. He showered her with gifts, bought her everything she wanted, gave her a life of luxury that most women would only dream of. But Emma wasn't satisfied. She knew that once the money was in her hands, the man would no longer be useful. So, she began to take steps to ensure that when the time came, she would be free—and rich.

It started slowly. Emma had learned from her own childhood that vulnerability was a currency, and she used it to manipulate Gregory's growing affection into something more dangerous. She would feign illness, growing weaker with each passing day. Gregory, convinced that she was frail and fragile, became even more obsessed with her. She started taking small doses of medication, enough to make her look pale, dizzy, even faint. He was worried about her, of course, but Emma was careful. She kept him close, watching over her like a hawk.

It wasn't long before he started to make decisions for her—decisions that left him completely under her control. She would play the part of the innocent wife, pleading for his help in making her well again. And when the time was right, Emma made her move. She added a stronger poison to his nightly glass of whiskey, just enough to cause him to slip into unconsciousness. When he died in his sleep, it was ruled as natural causes—heart failure, nothing suspicious. Emma was devastated, of course, shedding just enough tears to make it believable. And in a month's time, she inherited everything—his fortune, his assets, his name.

Her second marriage came only a year after Gregory's death. This time, it was Henry, a wealthy entrepreneur who had made his fortune in tech. He was a few years older than Gregory had been, but just as easily charmed. Emma played the same game again, slipping into the role of the perfect wife—someone who needed him, who admired him, who seemed completely dependent on his every word. This time, however, she didn't wait as long to strike. Emma had become more skilled, more methodical. She had no interest in waiting for Henry to become sick. She knew that time was of the essence, that she needed to strike before he grew tired of her.

She began by isolating him, making him believe that his friends and family were just trying to take advantage of him. She convinced him that he needed to cut ties with his business partners, that his wealth and success were his alone to protect. The more she fed into his paranoia, the more he trusted her, and before long, he had sold off most of his assets, leaving Emma with more than enough to secure her next step.

The night Henry died, Emma was there to comfort him. She held his hand as his breath became shallow, his heart slowing to a stop. This time, there was no poison in his drink, no slow-acting substance to cause his death. This time, Emma took a more direct approach. A pillow pressed tightly against his face. She watched as the man she had manipulated for months struggled, tried to fight, but ultimately succumbed to the suffocation. She was careful, as always—no marks, no signs of trauma. When the police arrived, it was another case of natural causes, the strain of his business decisions causing too much stress. Emma's acting was flawless, and within weeks, his estate was signed over to her.

Emma was careful with her third marriage. By now, she knew how to move in and out of men's lives without leaving a trace. She had learned to be even more patient, to wait until her target was completely infatuated, until he believed she was the only thing that mattered. She married Adam, a man who had inherited a large sum from his family's investment firm. This time, however, she made sure he was a man with fewer ties to the outside world, a man who trusted her completely. She didn't need to manipulate him for long. He was easy to deceive, and within a few months, she had everything she needed.

But Adam was different. Adam didn't get sick. Adam didn't grow old and weak. He was healthy, full of life, and not prone to the subtle ailments that had plagued her previous husbands. Emma had to act quickly. The longer she waited, the more she risked him catching on. But there was one mistake Emma made that she had overlooked in her haste: Adam had kept his affairs in order, and when Emma killed him, his death would not be as easy to cover up as the others. Adam had left instructions for his estate to be investigated after his death, his will clear in its demands.

The night Adam died, it was like all the others—Emma carefully slipped into his room, whispered the words she had used so many times before, and pressed a pillow into his face. But as Adam struggled, his fingers gripping her arms in a final act of defiance, something shifted inside Emma. This time, it wasn't satisfaction she felt. It wasn't the relief of completing the job. It was fear. Fear that everything she had built—the lies, the manipulation—would be undone. And when Adam's body lay lifeless beneath her, Emma realized the full scope of her mistake.

She had grown too confident. The things she had done to others had caught up with her, and now there was no escape. She had never considered the weight of her actions until it was too late. Emma had used her beauty and charm to manipulate and kill, but in doing so, she had destroyed her own soul. The money, the power—it was all worthless now. There was no victory. There was only emptiness, and for the first time, Emma understood what it felt like to truly lose everything.

The authorities arrived the next day, ready to investigate Adam's death, and this time, Emma's perfect facade cracked. In the end, it wasn't the men she had killed who were her undoing. It was the illusion of control, the arrogance of thinking she could escape the consequences of her own actions.

The Last Pit Stop

The truck stop was the kind of place most people forgot about the moment they left. For the drivers, it was a necessary pit stop—a place to stretch, to refuel, to grab a quick bite. It had the smell of grease, coffee, and the hum of fluorescent lights that flickered just a bit too often. For the people who worked there, it was a life lived in the margins. Among the truckers and travelers, there were only a few that stood out. They were the regulars, those who came for the food, the beer, or sometimes, for something more—something unsaid.

Sarah had worked at the truck stop for over two years. She was a waitress, though she preferred the term "attendant." The word "waitress" always made her feel like she was part of something less significant. She had a certain way of moving between the tables, gliding in and out of conversations, flashing smiles that were just a little too bright, just a little too practiced. The truckers loved her. They loved the way she made them feel important, the way her laughter filled the empty space between their tired eyes. And they loved the way she never judged, never questioned. She listened, and that was all they needed.

But Sarah's life wasn't the simple one it appeared to be. While she served her meals, wiped down counters, and rang up coffee, her mind was somewhere else, carefully planning the next move. She didn't just serve food. She had other things on her agenda—things that the men didn't know they were a part of. There was a darkness inside Sarah, one that had grown over the years of seeing the same faces come and go, hearing the same stories of road-weary men seeking solace in a fleeting moment of company.

Some of the truckers she encountered were kind, decent men who were just trying to make a living. But others were different. Some of them were rude, dismissive, even lecherous. Sarah had learned early on to tolerate them, to pretend that their words didn't sting, that their unwanted advances didn't make her skin crawl. But there was a breaking point for everyone. Sarah had reached hers. She had begun to resent the way they treated her—how easily they saw her as nothing more than a stop on their journey, a face to serve them, to please them. They came and went, as if their existence was more important than hers.

And so, she began to watch them more closely. The ones who were too bold, too smug, too eager to believe they were entitled to her attention, became her targets. She started small, testing her boundaries. She would offer to walk them to their trucks, offer a little extra attention, something that could be misinterpreted as kindness. They would follow, their hands lingering too long on her back, their breath thick with alcohol and desire. That's when she'd lead them to the dark, quiet corners of the truck stop parking lot. The places no one ever really looked.

It wasn't hard to find the ones who were vulnerable—those who were already half-drunk or too tired to think straight. A smile, a gentle touch, and she had them. She had learned how to slip away unnoticed, how to make sure no one saw the way she lured them into the shadows. Once there, the power was hers.

She had learned to use knives. It started with small cuts, subtle but painful. A slice across the arm. A slash to the throat. She made sure they bled out, but in a way that wasn't immediate. She wanted them to feel the terror, to understand that they were powerless, just like she had been. And when they begged, when they cried for mercy, Sarah simply smiled and listened. It was the final act of control she had over them.

It became a routine. She never killed for the same reasons—sometimes it was a punishment, sometimes it was just a release. The thrill of the kill didn't come from the death itself but from the ability to erase someone's existence in an instant, to make them as insignificant as they had made her feel for so long. She had a system. The bodies were always hidden—covered in the layers of darkness, left in isolated spots where the lights never reached. The police never connected the dots. The disappearances were chalked up to the loneliness of the road, to the dangers of hitchhiking, to the transient nature of the trucker lifestyle. No one suspected the friendly waitress, the one who served coffee with a smile and always made sure they were comfortable.

But one day, things started to shift. A new driver came into the truck stop, his name was Jack. He wasn't like the others. He didn't ogle her or make crude comments. He didn't flirt, didn't stare. He was polite, distant, but still kind in a way that made Sarah feel something she hadn't felt in a long time—real curiosity. Jack had a quiet intensity about him, something that made Sarah think twice. She found herself watching him more than usual, wondering if he was different from the others, if he was the kind of man who might be worth her time.

It wasn't long before he asked her to join him for a drink after her shift. Sarah hesitated, unsure if this was another game, another act to play, but something about his calm demeanor, his way of not seeing her as a thing to be conquered, made her agree. They sat in the small diner, just talking about life on the road. Jack didn't press her for anything. There were no flirtations, no undercurrent of expectation. He was simply there, listening.

For the first time in years, Sarah found herself thinking about more than just the next kill. She found herself wondering if there was more to her life than the emptiness she had carved out for herself. But as the night went on, Sarah's old instincts began to stir. She couldn't help herself. She began to lead him, gently but decisively, to the parking lot, just like she had with all the others. But as they reached the dark corner where she had killed so many, Jack stopped.

"I know what you're doing," he said, his voice quiet but firm.

Sarah froze, her heart suddenly racing. "What do you mean?" she asked, her voice suddenly unsure.

Jack smiled, not with malice, but with understanding. "You think you can control me. You think you're in charge. But I've been watching you too. And I think it's time you realize you're not as powerful as you think."

For the first time, Sarah felt the weight of her own arrogance. She had chosen him because he didn't fit into the mold she had made for her victims. But in the end, she had underestimated him. Jack didn't need her. And in that moment, she realized just how much of her power had always been an illusion.

He stepped back, slowly, deliberately. "You're not the predator you think you are," he said, his eyes cold. "You're just as trapped as the rest of them."

And with that, Sarah understood the twisted truth. She had been running from herself, from her own emptiness. She had taken lives to fill a void, but all it had done was create an endless cycle of destruction. And in the end, she was just as lost as the men she had killed.

The Unseen

Tessa had always been drawn to the quiet ones. She wasn't the type to fall for flashy personalities or loud, commanding voices. No, she preferred the subtle, the hidden. She liked to watch from the edges, to observe without being noticed. And when she saw Michael for the first time, her instinct told her he was just the kind of man she had been searching for—an enigmatic figure whose world was just out of reach, yet somehow, close enough for her to slip inside.

Michael was everything she wanted: handsome, successful, and always impeccably dressed. He had the kind of charisma that didn't need to be loud. His presence was felt, even in a crowded room. She had seen him a few times in passing, at the café where she worked, but he never paid much attention to her. At least, not until one fateful afternoon when he lingered just a little longer than usual. They exchanged a few casual words, nothing special, but it was enough to spark something inside Tessa.

She was a patient woman. She understood the art of waiting. And so, she watched. She studied him from a distance, learning the rhythm of his life. She knew where he went, when he worked late, what kind of books he read. It didn't take long before she discovered the secret he had kept hidden—his marriage. His wife, Andrea, was beautiful, confident, and utterly unaware of the woman who watched her husband so closely. Tessa had always admired Andrea from afar. She knew that she could never be her, but that didn't stop her from wanting what Andrea had. The thought of being in Michael's life, being the one to fill the empty spaces Andrea could never reach, consumed Tessa.

But she couldn't just slip in unnoticed. She needed to remove the barriers between her and Michael, to make sure he would never look at another woman the way he looked at his wife. And so, she began to target the women who stood between her and him—those who came before her, those who claimed his attention for even a brief moment.

It started with Sophie, a woman Michael had been casually seeing before his marriage to Andrea. Sophie was quiet, sweet even, but she had the one thing Tessa needed: proximity. She worked at a nearby art gallery and had seen Michael a few times before. She was the first obstacle in Tessa's mind, the first woman she would have to eliminate.

Tessa wasn't a fool. She knew Sophie's routine well. She knew where Sophie walked every morning, when she took her lunch breaks, and which bus she took home. It was almost too easy. One day, Tessa followed Sophie out of the gallery, watching from a distance as she made her way down the street, heading toward her apartment. Tessa had no intentions of confrontation, no desire to even speak to her. She just needed to remove the woman from Michael's life completely. And so, as Sophie walked down the alley beside her building, Tessa quietly approached. The blade was sharp, the movement swift. A quick slash, and Sophie's life was drained away before she even had a chance to scream.

The authorities ruled it a robbery gone wrong, a tragedy that could happen to anyone. Michael was devastated by the loss of someone he had once cared about, but Tessa knew better. She knew that Sophie would never again pose a threat to her.

After Sophie's death, Tessa's confidence grew. She had succeeded, and no one was any the wiser. She began to grow bolder, watching Michael and Andrea's relationship even more closely. She had learned to disguise herself, to blend in. She would slip into their lives just long enough to create chaos, to get close to the edge, without ever being caught. And soon, there was another woman—a younger, attractive colleague of Michael's named Rachel, who had been making subtle advances toward him. She was the perfect target. Tessa followed Rachel to a late-night gathering at a local bar. Rachel was out with friends, laughing, unaware of the dark figure in the crowd watching her.

When the bar was closing, and Rachel stumbled out into the night air, Tessa was already waiting, lurking in the shadows. A second life was taken—this time, in a dark corner, a quick stab to the back. No one heard a thing. Rachel's body was dumped in an alley, her death blamed on a random act of violence.

Each kill made Tessa more certain that she was doing the right thing. Michael was growing closer to her in subtle ways, his wife none the wiser. And yet, there was one final piece to the puzzle—the woman who truly stood in Tessa's way. Andrea.

Tessa had watched Andrea for years now, and she knew that the final kill would be the hardest, the most difficult to pull off. But it was necessary. Andrea's beauty, her confidence, her place in Michael's life—all of it made Tessa feel like an outsider. She could never have what Andrea had, unless she made sure the path was clear. She knew the risks. She would need to be careful, more careful than ever before. But she had planned for this.

It took months for Tessa to learn Andrea's routine—what time she took her morning jogs, when she ran errands, when she had lunch with friends. And on the day she finally decided to strike, she knew exactly where Andrea would be—alone, at a secluded spot near the park, the place where she often went to clear her head. Tessa had a plan, a foolproof one. She had prepared for everything.

But when she confronted Andrea that afternoon, standing face to face in the quiet park, something unexpected happened. Andrea didn't scream. She didn't fight back. She didn't even flinch when Tessa moved toward her. Instead, she smiled. "You've been watching me for a long time, haven't you?" Andrea's voice was calm, almost soothing.

Tessa froze, confused. "What do you mean?"

Andrea chuckled softly. "I knew what you were doing. I always knew. You thought you were invisible, but I saw the way you looked at me, the way you watched my husband. I knew something was wrong the moment Sophie disappeared."

Tessa's heart pounded in her chest. "No. You—how could you—?"

Andrea took a step closer, her smile never wavering. "You see, I've been playing this game too. You're not the only one with secrets."

And just like that, the woman she had tried to destroy—Andrea—revealed the truth: she had known all along, and had been playing her own long game, using Tessa's obsession against her. Tessa, the stalker, the killer, had been manipulated without even realizing it. The very thing she sought to take from Andrea, her life, was now at risk, because in the end, the woman she thought she could never be was the one who had been controlling the entire narrative from the start.

The Final Session

Dr. Miranda Holt was highly regarded in her field. A licensed therapist with a prestigious private practice, she had worked tirelessly to build a reputation as a skilled listener, a guiding hand for the troubled souls who came to her door. Her clients were often high-profile individuals—successful professionals, executives, artists—who sought her expertise to untangle the messes in their lives. They trusted her, confided in her, believing she was their key to self-discovery. They had no idea that, for Miranda, the path to enlightenment she offered was not one of healing, but one of control.

Miranda believed that true enlightenment came not through forgiveness or healing, but through release. Her patients were all weighed down by the burdens of guilt, regret, and pain—issues that she believed could only be resolved through confession, and ultimately, through death. She saw herself as a kind of spiritual guide, leading her patients to the ultimate freedom. She had never voiced these beliefs to anyone, of course. To the outside world, she was simply a compassionate, dedicated professional, committed to helping people find peace with their pasts. But inside, Miranda saw herself as a purifier, a necessary agent of fate.

Each new patient was an opportunity for her to continue her work. She would bring them in, use her soothing voice and calming presence to make them feel safe, secure in the space she had created. Then, like a spider waiting in the web, she would draw out their darkest secrets. She would coax confessions from them, gently, skillfully, making them believe they were purging themselves of their sins.

For Miranda, each confession was a step closer to freedom. Once they had unburdened themselves, once they had shared their deepest regrets, they were ready for the final step. She would offer them peace, a release from the suffering they had carried. But release, for Miranda, was not about helping them live. It was about helping them transcend. She believed that death was the final release from their earthly burdens, a way for them to finally reach true enlightenment.

It had begun with small acts—subtle manipulations that she justified as part of her therapeutic process. For a client like Alan, a successful businessman with a strained marriage, Miranda used his guilt over his infidelity to guide him toward what she saw as his ultimate truth. She had listened patiently as he described the affair, his voice trembling with shame, and she had whispered the words that would break him further. "You must face your consequences," she told him softly. "You must embrace the truth." It didn't take much to push him over the edge. One night, after a particularly intense session, she offered him a glass of water laced with a mild sedative. By the time he passed out on the couch, she was already preparing the final steps. Alan's death was staged to look like a heart attack, his body left in the comfort of his own home.

The police were baffled by his sudden death. His family, devastated by his loss, mourned him deeply, unaware that he had been led to his final fate by the very person who was supposed to help him. Miranda saw Alan's passing as a success. He had reached enlightenment, as she had hoped. He had been cleansed of his guilt in the most permanent of ways. And she could move on to the next one.

Her practice grew in popularity. More clients sought her expertise, eager to unravel their complex lives and find peace. Miranda was revered for her skill in guiding her patients to catharsis, her ability to unlock their deepest emotions. She cultivated this image of herself as a compassionate healer, someone who understood the complexities of human nature. But with each new confession, she grew more detached, more convinced that she was doing the world a service by relieving her patients of their burdens. She saw herself as a kind of martyr, selflessly helping others to transcend their pain—by any means necessary.

It wasn't until Lily came to her that Miranda's beliefs were tested. Lily was a young woman in her twenties, a brilliant artist whose paintings had been gaining recognition in the art world. But Lily was haunted by memories of her childhood—by the death of her mother, by her inability to live up to the expectations of her family. She came to Miranda for guidance, for relief from the overwhelming grief that seemed to define her every waking moment.

Miranda felt an immediate connection with Lily. Her vulnerability, her deep-seated guilt, spoke to something inside of Miranda. Lily had never truly forgiven herself for the choices she had made in her past, especially the estrangement from her mother before she passed. It was the perfect setup for Miranda's process. She could already feel the familiar pull, the growing sense of power that came from having someone like Lily under her influence.

But as the sessions went on, something shifted. Lily wasn't like the others. She didn't break down the way Miranda expected. She didn't give in easily to the guilt and shame that Miranda had so expertly drawn out of her clients before. Instead, Lily began to question everything. She began to ask Miranda about her methods, about the true purpose of her therapy. "You say you help people to face their demons," Lily once asked, "but what happens when those demons are too big? When the darkness is so overwhelming, there's no coming back?"

Miranda wasn't used to being questioned like this. She had always controlled the sessions, guided her patients in the direction she believed they should go. But Lily's resistance made Miranda uneasy. The more she pushed, the more Lily pulled away. She started to ask harder questions, questions that rattled Miranda's carefully constructed narrative. "What happens when someone can't forgive themselves? When the pain is so deep that it's too much to bear?" Lily's eyes searched Miranda's face, as though she could see through her, as though she could sense the darkness that Miranda had buried inside.

For the first time, Miranda felt a crack in her own belief system. Lily was supposed to be another success story, another victim of the past who would find release through confession. But Lily didn't need to confess. Lily needed something else, something Miranda couldn't provide.

One night, after another tense session, Miranda decided it was time to offer Lily the "release" she had offered so many others. She made the same preparations—sedatives, a glass of water, the final act. But as Lily drank the water, her eyes filled with an unexpected sadness, and Miranda saw something she had never expected: fear.

Lily looked at her, and for the first time, Miranda felt the full weight of what she had been doing. "I don't need your help," Lily whispered, her voice shaking. "I never did. I don't need you to free me."

Miranda's hand froze mid-air as she prepared the syringe. Lily had seen through her. She had seen that Miranda wasn't helping anyone. She wasn't guiding them to peace. She was killing them to fulfill her own twisted need for control.

Lily's death was ruled a suicide, just like the others. But this time, there was no sense of satisfaction for Miranda, no feeling of completion. There was only the horrifying realization that, in trying to save others, she had been the one who needed saving all along.

The Cut of Fate

Vivian had always been good with her hands. From a young age, she had understood the power of touch, the way a well-placed gesture could transform a person. As a child, she would run her fingers through her mother's hair, pulling and tugging until it fell perfectly in place. Her mother had always appreciated it, though Vivian's small hands sometimes fumbled with the knots. But Vivian quickly learned—there was a rhythm to it, a magic in the way a simple comb could restore order to a person's chaotic world. She had an eye for beauty, an understanding of shapes, textures, and the way light danced through hair.

It was no surprise, then, that she became a hairdresser. She spent years perfecting her craft, opening her own salon in a cozy corner of the city. Her shop became a haven for women, and even some men, who wanted not just a haircut but an experience. Vivian wasn't just a stylist—she was a confidante, a listener. Clients sat in her chair and revealed their deepest fears, desires, and insecurities. She made them feel seen, important, and beautiful. They trusted her with their looks, but what they didn't realize was that Vivian was taking far more than that.

The power she held in her hands, the way she could shape and change someone's appearance with a few snips of the scissors, was intoxicating. But it wasn't enough for Vivian. She began to realize that she could control more than just the surface. She could change lives. A bad haircut, a subtle change in style—these things could alter someone's mood, their confidence, their decisions. And if she could do that, what else could she manipulate?

It started with Sara, a regular client who always had the same requests: a trim here, a little volume there, never straying too far from her comfort zone. But Sara's life wasn't as simple as her hair. She worked in a high-pressure job, had a strained marriage, and often confided in

Vivian about her feelings of inadequacy. Vivian listened, offering words of reassurance, always with a smile. But one day, as she worked the scissors through Sara's hair, a thought crept into her mind. What if she could help Sara make a change? Not just in her appearance, but in her entire life?

Vivian began to experiment, adding small touches of sabotage. She'd ask Sara about her relationship, about the things that bothered her husband. And when Sara complained about how much her husband drank, Vivian would gently suggest remedies—a special herbal tea here, a supplement there. But these weren't just benign suggestions. They were the beginning of something darker. Vivian began to slip mild sedatives into the teas she prepared for Sara, watching as her energy slowly drained away. Over time, Sara grew more exhausted, more distant. Her marriage crumbled under the weight of her confusion, her lack of focus. Vivian smiled to herself each time she saw Sara's sad eyes in the mirror, watching the unraveling of a life she had subtly orchestrated.

Vivian didn't stop there. The more she controlled, the more she craved. There were other clients, too—people who came to her with their problems, their doubts, their heartbreaks. They trusted her, and she used that trust to manipulate them. Emily, a young woman with a bright future ahead, came in one day, thrilled about an upcoming job promotion. Vivian congratulated her, but she also saw a vulnerability. Emily was too trusting, too eager to please. Over the next few weeks, Vivian began to slip in suggestions—subtle remarks about how her boss might be taking advantage of her, how some people in the office were gossiping behind her back. The poison wasn't just in the water she gave her or the gossip she subtly fed. It was in the way she helped Emily sabotage her own career, pushing her to confront her boss with accusations that were unwarranted. Emily lost her job. She hadn't realized it, but Vivian had made sure of it.

As Vivian's influence grew, so did her satisfaction. She began to see herself as something more than just a stylist. She was a creator, an architect of lives, pulling the strings behind the scenes. But with each victory, the power she wielded began to feel hollow. She no longer found joy in simply cutting hair. She wanted more. She wanted total control.

It wasn't long before she targeted Rachel, a woman in her early forties who had recently gone through a divorce. Rachel was a regular at the salon, but her insecurity had grown since the breakup. She always asked for the latest trends, trying desperately to hold onto her youth, but nothing seemed to work. Vivian took an interest in Rachel's self-esteem, listening patiently as she vented about feeling unattractive, unlovable. Vivian reassured her, but in a way that felt calculated. She made sure Rachel was aware of her beauty, but only in comparison to others, always implying that she needed something more to be truly happy. One day, after a particularly lengthy session, Vivian offered Rachel a "special treatment"—a hair dye that promised to brighten her appearance, make her feel rejuvenated.

The dye, of course, was laced with something else. A substance that wouldn't be immediately noticeable but would slowly begin to alter her health—an allergen, carefully chosen to provoke an immune response. Rachel began to feel off, dizzy, pale. Her visits became more frequent as she sought solutions for the mysterious illness, all the while unaware of Vivian's hand in her suffering. Her life began to crumble. She lost weight, became withdrawn, and her confidence faded, all while Vivian whispered words of sympathy and "advice."

The turning point came when a young woman named Claire walked into Vivian's salon one rainy afternoon. She was fresh-faced, full of life, and eager for change. She had just moved to town and was looking for a new look, a new start. There was something in her eyes, a vulnerability that was too familiar. As Vivian combed through her hair, she began to plan. Claire was perfect. A blank slate, full of potential.

Vivian could shape her life, just as she had with the others. But this time, something felt different. As Claire shared her story, her hopes, her ambitions, Vivian realized how far she had fallen. She had done so much damage, ruined so many lives, all in the pursuit of something she couldn't even name.

Vivian felt a pang of something unfamiliar. Was it guilt? Regret? She couldn't be sure, but it was enough to make her pause. She set the scissors down, looking at Claire in the mirror, seeing the young woman's eyes reflect her own doubt.

"Maybe you don't need to change after all," Vivian said, her voice softer than it had been in years.

But Claire, unaware of the conflict stirring inside Vivian, smiled brightly. "Oh, I think I do. A fresh start, you know?"

Vivian had never felt more trapped. She had crafted the perfect life for herself, built on manipulation and lies, but now she was left facing the truth that she had become the very thing she hated—the person who controlled, who poisoned, who ruined. The final cut had come, not with scissors, but with a realization she couldn't escape.

As Claire left the salon, her bright future untouched by Vivian's influence, Vivian understood that she had never truly known the power she sought. It wasn't in the lives she had shaped, but in the one she had destroyed. And now, there was no way to undo what she had done to herself.

The Invisible Threads

Grace had always been a master of reinvention. It wasn't that she was born with any particular skills or natural charisma, but she had something far more valuable: the ability to disappear. She learned early on that blending into the background was the key to survival. She was quiet, unassuming, the kind of person who could slip into a room and not be noticed, who could enter a conversation and leave without leaving a trace. People rarely paid attention to her. They didn't need to.

The internet, however, offered a new kind of anonymity—a chance to become whoever she wanted to be. Grace wasn't the first to discover the power of online spaces. Chat rooms, social media, forums—places where people gathered to share their stories, their struggles, their secrets—became her domain. She could reinvent herself with every new screen name, every new persona. And she did. The fragile, self-deprecating woman who opened up to strangers about her hardships and fears became the perfect mask for the real Grace. She would weave elaborate tales of loss, betrayal, and heartache. She would talk about her failed marriages, her abusive past, the crippling loneliness that haunted her. All of it was a lie, of course, but it was a lie people wanted to believe.

At first, it was harmless. Grace didn't need to meet anyone face-to-face. The words were enough. But as she built these online relationships, as she made friends in these virtual spaces, she started to crave something more. She began to realize that these women—these strangers who poured out their hearts to her—trusted her. And Grace, with her quiet charm and seemingly endless sympathy, was able to draw them in.

She began to target the vulnerable ones, the women who wore their pain on their sleeves, who looked for solace in the virtual arms of a stranger. Grace knew how to comfort them, to make them feel seen, heard, understood. But she also knew something else: they were perfect for what she really wanted. She wasn't looking for sympathy or understanding; she was looking for something far darker. She wanted to be someone else, and to do that, she needed to erase someone else.

The first woman Grace killed was Sarah. Sarah was a mother of two, living in a small town, struggling with an abusive relationship. She and Grace met in a support group chat. Sarah's messages were filled with heartbreak and longing, and Grace responded with the right amount of empathy. They spent weeks talking, and during that time, Grace found out everything—Sarah's fears, her hopes, her address, even the names of her children. Sarah trusted Grace implicitly, seeing her as a kindred spirit, someone who understood her pain.

Grace lured her into a false sense of security. She told Sarah that she was coming to visit, that they could meet in person, talk face-to-face. It would be a new beginning, Grace promised her, a way for them to heal together. Sarah, vulnerable and hopeful, agreed.

When Sarah opened the door to Grace, she had no idea that the woman standing in front of her wasn't the person she had been talking to online. The smile was different. The eyes were colder. But Sarah, like so many others, didn't see the warning signs. She was too desperate to believe the lie. Grace stepped inside, and before Sarah could understand what was happening, she had already turned her back, and Grace had the advantage. The life drained from Sarah's body quickly, too quickly, as the knife Grace had slipped into her hand went to work.

Afterward, Grace didn't panic. She calmly rifled through Sarah's belongings, took her wallet, her phone, her identification. She wiped the apartment clean of fingerprints, leaving no trace of her presence. Then she began her real work. She became Sarah.

It was easy enough. She used the stolen phone to send messages to Sarah's friends and family, telling them that Sarah had left town, that she was going to start fresh, away from the pain of her past. No one questioned it. Sarah's social media profiles were updated, her life remade, and Grace slipped into the role seamlessly. She wore Sarah's face, lived her life, and no one was the wiser.

But Sarah wasn't the last. There were others—women who poured their hearts out in online chats, women who needed someone to listen, someone to offer comfort. Grace continued her deception, each new woman offering another opportunity to assume a new identity. She grew more confident, more practiced. The lies she told were as easy to slip into as the clothes she wore.

But with each new identity, something inside Grace shifted. The lines between who she was and who she pretended to be blurred. She started to lose track of the women she had killed, the lives she had stolen. It didn't matter. They were all the same to her. The thrill was in the deception, in the control, in becoming someone else and leaving the wreckage behind.

Her final victim was Megan. Megan was different from the others. She had been a social worker, helping others who had been through trauma. Her past was filled with abuse, but she had risen above it. Grace knew she had to be careful with Megan. She had built a reputation online as someone who could handle anything, who had seen it all. She would be harder to deceive, harder to manipulate. But Grace was clever. She used Megan's compassion to pull her in, used her sense of duty to draw her closer.

It didn't take long before Megan was hooked. They shared stories of their painful pasts, their failures, their regrets. Megan, who had spent her life helping others, finally found someone who seemed to need her in return. Grace played the role perfectly, making Megan feel essential, like she was the one person who could help her.

Grace invited Megan to meet her, in person, just like she had done with the others. Megan agreed, believing it was another step in their journey to help each other. When Megan showed up at the meeting place, Grace was waiting, but something was off. Megan, still trusting, stepped forward—just as Grace struck. But this time, Grace hesitated.

Megan wasn't like the others. Megan wasn't just another victim to be discarded. She had seen through the cracks in Grace's persona. Before Grace could make her move, Megan grabbed her wrist. "I know who you are," Megan said, her voice calm, almost resigned. "I know what you've done."

Grace froze, shock crawling through her veins. How could Megan know? How could she have figured it out?

Megan smiled softly, her grip loosening. "I've been watching you too. I know your game, and I've already sent everything to the authorities."

The trap that Grace had woven so carefully for others had now ensnared her. Megan had turned the tables, using the same manipulations Grace had used on her victims. And as Grace was taken into custody, her carefully crafted identity dissolved, leaving her exposed, nothing but a shadow of the lies she had lived.

Grace had become the victim of her own deceptions, a lesson in how easily trust could be exploited—and how the truth always catches up, no matter how many identities one hides behind.

The Widowmaker

Clara lived in a world of quiet privilege. She knew exactly what she wanted and had learned how to get it: the luxuries, the security, the peace of mind that came with knowing she was always taken care of. She wasn't born into wealth, but she had made her way there through careful calculation, through choices that others would have called cold or even immoral. But to Clara, it was simply strategy. She understood the power that came with being desired, with being the object of someone's affection—especially when that someone had a lifetime of wealth and security to offer.

Her choice of men was deliberate. She never went for those her age. They were too energetic, too independent. They wanted too much in return. No, Clara preferred older men, those who had worked for decades, who had accumulated pensions, savings, and property. They were often widowed or lonely, looking for a second chance at love, a companion to ease their final years. They were vulnerable, desperate even. And Clara knew exactly how to make them feel special.

Her latest target was Charles, a retired lawyer in his late seventies. He was rich, with a portfolio full of real estate and investments. He had no children, no family to speak of, and he had been widowed for five years. He had met Clara at a local charity event, where she had played the role of the demure, elegant woman in her forties who still had a touch of youth in her eyes. He was smitten instantly, charmed by her soft voice, the way she listened intently, the way she made him feel like the most important person in the room. Within weeks, Clara had maneuvered herself into his life, becoming his constant companion. She was everything he wanted, everything he thought he needed.

They married quietly, with only a handful of close friends attending. Clara by his side for everything—his doctor's appointments, his dinners with old friends, and his slow, painful decline. But while Charles grew older and weaker, Clara became more vibrant, more alive with every passing day. She made sure to keep up appearances, to show the world how much she adored him. She was the perfect wife, a picture of devotion, even as her true intentions simmered beneath the surface.

Charles had health problems—nothing too serious, but enough to require frequent doctor visits. High blood pressure, diabetes, some memory issues that made him forget things he once took for granted. Clara made sure he stayed on top of his medication, always making sure he took his pills, his vitamins, his supplements. But what Charles didn't know was that Clara had her own brand of medicine in mind—medicine that would make him more docile, more compliant. At first, she simply adjusted his prescriptions, adding a little extra dose here, a little extra dose there. Just enough to make him sluggish, tired, easily manipulated. He didn't question it. He trusted her completely.

As the months went by, Charles's health began to deteriorate more rapidly. Clara made sure he didn't notice the changes. She carefully monitored his routines, ensuring that no one suspected anything was amiss. She would often take him out for walks, make sure he was socializing, acting as though she was the loving wife who cared deeply for his well-being. But each step, each meal, each drug-laced cup of tea brought him closer to the end. She knew exactly when to act, when to push him just far enough to make his heart give out.

The day Charles finally died was as anticlimactic as she had planned. He had a sudden heart attack while reading the newspaper, sitting in his favorite chair by the window. Clara, sitting across from him, had already seen the signs—she had pushed him far enough, and now it was time for him to go. His last moments were spent gasping for air, his eyes wide with confusion, but Clara's face never wavered. She rushed to his side, calling 911, crying out in disbelief, even as she knew exactly what had happened.

The police came, the paramedics came, and they all did their jobs, concluding that it was an unfortunate but natural death. Clara mourned, of course, in the way a widow is expected to mourn. She threw herself into the funeral arrangements, played the grieving wife, and within weeks, she had everything she had set her sights on. His house, his savings, his pension—everything he had worked for was now hers.

But Clara wasn't done. She didn't simply want his wealth. She wanted to keep the game going. She wanted to continue using the power she had learned to wield over these men, over their desires, their weaknesses. And so, she moved on to her next target.

It didn't take long for Clara to find another older man, another lonely soul in need of companionship. This one was Edward, a widower in his early eighties, with a similar background—wealthy, but without anyone left to care for him. He was drawn to Clara just like the others. She knew all the right things to say, how to make him feel young again, how to make him feel loved. Clara repeated the cycle with him, gaining his trust, his affection.

But this time, something was different. Edward was sharper than Charles had been. He had seen it all, lived through more than his fair share of betrayals and heartbreaks. He wasn't easily fooled. He noticed that Clara was always the one in control, always the one who made the decisions. He was suspicious, at first, of how quickly she moved into his life, but he was old, and the loneliness gnawed at him.

One night, after a dinner with friends, Clara went to Edward's house to administer the final dose. But this time, when she approached him with the drink she had laced with the same sedatives, Edward stopped her. He had seen through her act. His sharp eyes glinted with understanding as he looked at her, almost amused.

"You think I don't know what you're doing?" Edward said, his voice weak but firm. "You're just like the others."

Clara froze. She had always been the one in control. She had always been the one who decided when and how the story ended. But this time, it seemed the ending wasn't going to come the way she planned.

Edward had known all along. He had seen the pattern, recognized the signs. Clara had underestimated him, just like she had underestimated every other man she had manipulated. But it was too late to back out now. She couldn't let him expose her.

In that moment, Clara realized something she had never accounted for. She had been playing the game for so long, manipulating others into doing her bidding, that she had forgotten one crucial detail—everyone has a breaking point, a moment when they can see through the façade. And now, it was her turn to face the consequences of her actions.

Edward smiled weakly, watching as Clara's expression shifted. She realized then that the game was over, and she had become the one who was played. The irony of it was clear now—just as she had killed to claim their lives and their wealth, someone else had claimed hers.

The Fate Weaver

Lena Holloway had always been good at reading people. It was a skill that had served her well in life, and she had honed it until it was almost second nature. She could see the way a person's eyes darted when they were lying, the subtle shift in their posture when they were hiding something. She understood the human condition better than most, but it wasn't just about reading people—it was about using that knowledge to manipulate them. She had learned that trick early, growing up in a family that relied on charm and deceit to get by.

By the time Lena was in her thirties, she had found her calling. She set up shop as a psychic, a fortune-teller, someone who could peer into the future and give people guidance. Of course, it wasn't real. It was all smoke and mirrors—tarot cards, crystal balls, incense, and the careful use of words. She would tell her clients what they wanted to hear, manipulating their fears and desires to weave stories that felt like truth. They came to her broken, searching for answers, and Lena was happy to provide them—answers that often led them to make decisions that would bring them closer to her ultimate goal.

She started with small cons—telling people they needed to take risks, or that their destiny lay in the hands of someone they knew, prompting them to make decisions that benefited her. But soon, Lena grew bored with just scamming people for small amounts of cash. She wanted more. She wanted power. She realized that by manipulating their fears, she could drive them to do anything. And if she could drive them to do anything, then perhaps she could bring them to a place where their fate was sealed—a place where death would be her final prediction.

It wasn't long before she began her true work. Her first victim was Angela, a young woman in her late twenties who came to Lena in a state of panic. She had recently broken up with her boyfriend and was struggling to make ends meet. Angela was desperate for answers, her mind full of what-ifs, uncertainties, and fears about the future. Lena saw the vulnerability in her immediately. She could tell that Angela was not just seeking guidance, but something deeper—something that could be used.

Lena began with her usual routine. She told Angela that her future was dark and full of uncertainty, but that she could see a way out—a way to avoid the impending disaster. Lena spoke cryptically, hinting at a man in Angela's life who might betray her. She planted the seeds of doubt, just enough to make Angela feel like her ex-boyfriend was still lurking in the shadows. She told her that she needed to be cautious, that someone close to her was not to be trusted. But then, in the same breath, Lena told her that the only way to rid herself of this threat was to confront him directly, to make a bold move. She told her the confrontation would give Angela the closure she so desperately needed.

Angela, full of fear and uncertainty, followed Lena's advice. She arranged a meeting with her ex-boyfriend, intending to finally end the tension between them. It was late at night, and Lena had convinced Angela that the final confrontation was best held in private. When Angela arrived at the secluded spot they had arranged, Lena was watching from a distance, knowing that things would go exactly as planned.

The confrontation escalated quickly. Angela, fueled by doubt and fear, began accusing her ex of things that weren't entirely true. The argument grew violent. In the chaos, Angela's ex lashed out, and the encounter ended in a tragic accident. Angela was left dead in the street, and her ex was arrested for involuntary manslaughter.

Lena claimed she had seen it all in her visions, that she had "predicted" the outcome, and as she comforted Angela's family, Lena made sure to subtly reinforce the idea that Angela's death had been inevitable. The authorities were quick to rule the death an accident, and Lena quietly collected her payment—a large sum from the grieving family, desperate for closure.

But Lena didn't stop there. She grew more daring with each success, targeting those who came to her, looking for help, for guidance. She would find the weakest, the most desperate, and manipulate them into situations where they would eventually meet their demise. She fed their paranoia, their fear, and convinced them that their paths were doomed unless they followed her advice.

Her next victim was Veronica, an older woman in her fifties who was battling breast cancer. Veronica came to Lena seeking solace, hoping that the psychic would tell her there was hope, that she could beat the disease. Lena, with her practiced sympathy, told Veronica that her illness was part of a greater cosmic struggle, that the disease had come into her life to test her strength. But Lena also told her that Veronica's fate was already written. She told her that she would have to make a bold, risky move in order to survive—a move that would give her back control.

Lena encouraged Veronica to refuse traditional treatment, promising that a spiritual cleansing would rid her body of the disease. Veronica, desperate to believe Lena's words, followed her advice, abandoning her chemotherapy and opting for alternative methods Lena had suggested. The cancer worsened, and Veronica's condition deteriorated quickly. She died within months, and once again, Lena was there, comforting the family, claiming that Veronica's death had been part of her destiny all along.

Lena's reputation grew. People came to her from all walks of life, searching for answers, and she fed on their fears, shaping their lives in ways they couldn't comprehend. Each death was more satisfying than the last—an intricate tapestry of manipulation and power woven together by her carefully planned words.

But it wasn't until she met Emily that things began to unravel. Emily was different. She came to Lena not seeking answers, but questioning everything. She had heard rumors about Lena's predictions, her advice, her uncanny ability to "foretell" the future.

But Emily wasn't afraid of Lena. Instead, she was intrigued by her. She didn't believe in the supernatural, and she didn't believe that Lena could really help her. But she came anyway, hoping to understand the woman who had been feeding on others' vulnerabilities.

Lena, sensing that Emily was not as easy to manipulate, tried her usual tricks—feeding her fears, telling her she was on the verge of something terrible. But Emily wasn't fooled. She listened, but she didn't buy it. When Lena suggested that Emily might be in danger, Emily simply smiled. "You don't predict my fate, Lena," she said, her voice steady and unwavering. "You create it."

Lena's heart skipped a beat. Something in Emily's words made her feel exposed, vulnerable for the first time in years. Emily left that day, and Lena's confidence began to crack. How could someone so calm, so sure of herself, see through her charade so easily?

A few weeks later, Lena's life started to unravel. The people she had manipulated began to ask questions. The family members of her victims started to connect the dots, noticing the odd patterns. Emily had begun to dig, quietly investigating the women who had died after seeking Lena's guidance. She had been right. Lena had been the one creating their fate, not predicting it.

In the end, it wasn't fate that came for Lena—it was her own lies catching up to her. The police arrived one evening to arrest her, and as she was taken away, she realized the dark truth: the one she had manipulated most was herself. She had woven a web of deceit so tightly around others, she hadn't seen it slowly tightening around her own throat.

The lesson was simple: even the most skilled manipulators, the ones who think they control fate, can become prisoners of their own making.

The Homecoming

Lena had always known that she was different. Raised in a religious cult, she had been taught to believe that the world outside their small compound was corrupt and evil, a place where the faithful would surely falter if they ever stepped foot in it. The elders of the cult, especially Father Elias, had instilled in her an unwavering sense of duty to the cause. To them, she was nothing more than an instrument of their vision—someone to mold, to control, to use for their greater purpose. For most of her life, Lena had been little more than a shadow, a figure in the background, obedient to the whims of those in charge. But that had all changed the day she finally escaped.

It wasn't easy. The cult had its eyes everywhere, its surveillance tight. They had always monitored the thoughts of the children, making sure that they never strayed from the teachings of Father Elias. Lena's escape was not a moment of triumph—it was a quiet, desperate act, fueled by the rage and resentment she had bottled up for years. She had waited until the compound had fallen asleep, then snuck through the back gate, a small bag of belongings clutched tightly in her hands. She didn't look back. The freedom she felt was fleeting, but it was hers.

For years, Lena lived on the fringes of society, trying to adjust to a world she had been kept from for so long. She learned quickly that the real world wasn't as forgiving as she had been taught. She worked odd jobs, kept to herself, never allowing anyone to get too close. The trauma of her upbringing never truly left her. There was always a voice in her head telling her she was worthless, telling her that she didn't deserve anything. But over time, she found her strength. She rebuilt herself, piece by piece, as she learned the art of survival.

But no matter how much she tried to move on, there was one thing that remained—her anger. The people she had known in the cult, the ones who had been like family to her, had abandoned her without a second thought. When she left, no one came after her. No one asked where she had gone. She was just gone, erased, as if she had never mattered in the first place.

It wasn't long before the memories started to twist into something darker. Lena began to plot. She had spent years studying the psychology of manipulation, learning how to manipulate others in ways that would make the cult leaders proud. She had learned to use the very skills they had taught her against them. And now, she had a plan.

It started with the messages. Lena knew how to contact the former members of the cult without revealing her identity. She used anonymous online forums, fake accounts, and burner phones. She knew how they thought, how they had been conditioned to believe that they were the chosen ones, special and superior to everyone else. The cult had always preached the idea of purity, of being free from sin. Lena knew that by appealing to their desire for redemption, she could draw them back in.

The invitation was simple: "It's time to come home."

She knew exactly what to say, how to speak to each of them individually. The former cult members, scattered across the country, would receive her messages one by one. Each note was personalized, just enough to make them believe it was from Father Elias himself, calling them back to the fold. Lena painted a picture of salvation, of unity, of the old days when they had felt invincible together. But what they didn't know was that this homecoming would be their last.

She had arranged everything meticulously. The old compound, long abandoned, was now the setting for her trap. Lena had hired a small group of trusted people to help her secure the place—people who didn't know the full story, people who only knew that they were getting paid to keep the area secure. She had taken extra care to make sure everything appeared normal, even sacred. The place had to feel like a return to something familiar, a place where the past could be relived in perfect harmony.

As the cult members began to arrive, they were greeted with familiar sights—old symbols, the scent of incense in the air. Lena had orchestrated every detail to make them feel like they were stepping back into their old lives. There was Father Elias' old chair, the one he used to sit in during meetings. There were candles lit in the shape of the sacred emblem they had always revered. It all felt like a reunion, like a resurrection of their past, and that's exactly what Lena wanted.

One by one, they came, and one by one, Lena welcomed them into the fold. She spoke to them softly, the same way Father Elias had spoken to her all those years ago. She assured them that they had made the right choice by returning, that this was their path to redemption. They followed her every word, just as they always had. But when they had all gathered in the center of the room, Lena's tone shifted. The warmth in her voice evaporated, replaced by a cold, detached certainty.

They had no idea that everything they had done had been in preparation for their final act.

Lena locked the doors behind them. The compound was now a cage, and she was the one in control. The faces of the men and women who had once been her family now looked uncertain, their eyes scanning the room, realizing that something wasn't right. But by then, it was too late. Lena had planned for this moment. She had studied their weaknesses, their fears. Each of them had been carefully chosen, their minds primed to trust her.

The gas began to seep in through the vents.

As the room filled with the suffocating, invisible substance, Lena stood in the center, watching them struggle. She had waited for this moment, this revenge for everything they had done to her. They had taught her to be obedient, to be silent, to endure. But she had learned their lesson well, and now she would show them what it felt like to be powerless.

The last of them fell to the ground, unconscious, their breaths shallow and labored. Lena moved slowly, methodically, as she set the compound on fire, the flames consuming everything. The last trace of the life they had forced on her was about to be erased, and she stood outside, watching the fire burn, feeling the heat on her face.

The lesson was simple: you can trap someone, control them, manipulate them, but in the end, there is always a price to pay. And in that moment, Lena realized that her vengeance had come at the cost of her own soul. But she didn't care. The past was gone, and with it, the people who had taken so much from her. She was free.

The Perfect Day

Natalie Whitaker was the kind of woman everyone adored. She had a warmth to her, an easy smile that made her clients feel like the most important people in the world. Running her own wedding planning business, *A Perfect Day*, she had established herself as one of the best in the city. From the moment a couple walked into her office, she made them feel seen, heard, and cherished. She knew exactly how to listen to their dreams and translate them into reality—a perfect ceremony, a flawless reception. Every detail was handled with grace, down to the smallest flower petal or the precise shade of white on the linens. Her clients raved about her, often recommending her to friends and family, their glowing testimonials plastered all over her website.

But beneath the flawless exterior, something darker simmered.

Natalie didn't just plan weddings. She controlled them. She observed her couples closely, studying their dynamics, their personalities, their weaknesses. She made it her business to know everything—about their families, their histories, their past loves. Over the years, she had come to realize something unsettling. Some marriages, no matter how beautiful the ceremony or how grand the occasion, weren't meant to last. Some people, in her opinion, didn't deserve the love they had found. They were careless with it. They were reckless with their promises. And when she saw that, she took it upon herself to fix the problem.

It started small at first, little things that no one would ever notice. A well-placed word here, a subtle change there. She might whisper to a bride that her fiancé had been talking to his ex, plant a seed of doubt in her mind. She might "accidentally" double-book a venue or arrange for the caterers to be late. There were moments when the stress of wedding planning would push her clients into fits of anxiety, and she would smile softly, as if to soothe them, while secretly enjoying the chaos that began to unravel their perfect day.

But that was just the beginning. Natalie had grown tired of simply watching the weddings she orchestrated fall apart. She wanted more control. She wanted to eliminate the people she deemed unworthy, to erase them from the picture entirely.

Her first true act was a groom named Ben. Ben was wealthy, charming, and, by all outward appearances, completely in love with his bride, Claire. But Natalie had done her homework. She had learned about Ben's past—how he had cheated on a previous girlfriend, how he had a reputation for using people, for discarding them when they no longer suited him. Claire was sweet, innocent, and so incredibly devoted. But Ben had never been the right man for her. Natalie saw it in every glance he gave her, every dismissive word he said. He was unworthy of her love.

So, Natalie took matters into her own hands. She had the caterers prepare a special dish for Ben, a dish he was allergic to, something he had never mentioned to Claire. The night of the wedding, everything went smoothly—except for one thing. Ben's reaction to the food was instant. He started gasping for air, clutching his throat in a panic. Claire screamed, running to his side, but it was too late. The doctors later confirmed that it was anaphylactic shock, and Ben's life had ended in a matter of minutes.

Claire was devastated. She mourned Ben publicly, but Natalie was there, always a step ahead, comforting her, telling her that it was tragic but that everything would be okay. The sympathy was genuine, but the satisfaction in Natalie's heart was palpable. Ben's absence was a gift—one that would make Claire stronger, and one that would allow her to move on to someone more deserving of her love.

With each wedding, Natalie's confidence grew. She knew she had found her purpose. She began targeting grooms, and sometimes brides, whom she found lacking. Some were arrogant, others dishonest, and some simply unworthy of the perfect marriages they had dreamed about. She would continue to offer her services, always with a smile, always with the perfect advice, but behind the scenes, she was creating chaos—fomenting distrust, encouraging insecurity, and, when necessary, administering a final, irreversible act.

One particular wedding stands out in Natalie's memory. It was a high-profile affair—Samantha and Lucas, a stunning couple with a storybook romance. Samantha was beautiful, poised, and successful. Lucas was handsome, kind, and charismatic. They were perfect for each other, or so it seemed. But Natalie saw something in Lucas—something that made her uneasy. He was too perfect, too eager to please. And when Natalie dug deeper into his past, she uncovered a dark secret. Lucas had been involved in a hit-and-run accident years ago, one that had left a man in critical condition, and Lucas had never taken responsibility for it. The guilt weighed on him, though he had managed to bury it, and he had never confessed to anyone.

Natalie knew what had to be done. She invited him for a private meeting under the pretext of discussing last-minute details. She listened to his confessions, coaxed the truth from him, and once she had everything she needed, she manipulated his emotions. She told him that confessing his past to Samantha would ruin their perfect future, that the guilt would eat him alive. She made him believe that there was no way forward unless he dealt with his past. She even arranged for him to "accidentally" encounter the man from the hit-and-run at a local bar, knowing that the confrontation would send Lucas into a state of panic.

When the wedding day arrived, Natalie's careful planning paid off. Lucas was a wreck. He couldn't bear the guilt, couldn't face the woman he had promised to love forever. The ceremony was chaotic, the vows never completed. Lucas was unable to say the words, unable to follow through on his promises. In a frenzy, he fled the scene, and in his state of mind, he ran straight into traffic. The crash that followed was fatal.

Samantha was left heartbroken, her dreams shattered. And once again, Natalie was there, consoling her, whispering that it wasn't meant to be. She reassured Samantha that she would find love again, that everything had happened for a reason. The grief was palpable, but Natalie's satisfaction was undeniable.

It was only after years of orchestrating these tragic endings that Natalie finally stopped to reflect. She had built a business, a reputation, and a life around her manipulations, all under the guise of helping others. But as she looked at the ruined lives she had left behind, she realized that she had become a puppet master, but no one was pulling her strings. She had no control, no love, and no future of her own. She had been so focused on destroying others' happiness that she had forgotten to build her own.

And so, she continued, always one step ahead, orchestrating the deaths she believed were necessary. The weddings she arranged would always end in tragedy, but for Natalie, the satisfaction of her control was all that mattered.

The Park Bench Killer

Clara had always been drawn to the loneliness of public parks. There was something about the quiet space, the open air, and the soft hum of people moving through their day that soothed her. She would sit on the worn benches, pretending to read a book or watch the passing joggers, but her eyes were always scanning, always searching for the ones who looked lost. She had learned long ago that the lonely ones were the easiest to find. They were the ones who were open to conversation, the ones who looked like they had no one else to talk to, and it was those very people Clara was drawn to.

It was in the solitude of a park that she found a kind of power. As she wandered the grounds, her fingers grazing the peeling paint of benches and the rough bark of trees, she would smile at the ones who caught her attention. The middle-aged man reading the newspaper on his lunch break, the elderly woman feeding pigeons, the man sitting on a bench staring into space, eyes vacant, lost in thought. Each of them was like a puzzle, their lives spilling out through small signs—the crinkle of their eyes, the way their shoulders slumped, or the way they never quite made eye contact. These were people whose lives had become too quiet, too empty, and Clara knew that a few well-placed words could open them up to anything.

Her method was simple. She would sit next to them on the bench, her presence always soft and non-threatening. She'd give a knowing glance or ask a question that seemed casual—something that wouldn't alarm them. "I always love the smell of fresh grass in the morning," she might say, or "It's funny how the sound of birds always reminds me of my grandmother's house." She could always tell who would respond, and those who didn't simply weren't her type. But the ones who did—they were the ones she needed.

The first time it happened, she hadn't even planned it. She had sat beside a man named Mark, a man in his early forties, his hair thinning, his face creased with the marks of someone who had worked hard but hadn't seen much return for it. He had the look of someone whose life had lost its purpose, and Clara could feel the vulnerability radiating off him. He looked at her, hesitated for a moment, then began to speak. It was the kind of conversation that flowed easily, as though they had known each other for years. She let him talk, let him pour out his frustrations about a job that didn't appreciate him, about a failed marriage that had left him feeling hollow, about how he had been searching for something—anything—to give his life meaning.

And Clara, with the right combination of sympathy and interest, had made him believe that she understood, that she cared. She invited him to take a walk with her, to show him a more peaceful part of the park—a quiet, secluded path she knew would give her the perfect setting. Mark didn't hesitate. His eyes lit up with a sense of hope, of validation that someone, anyone, cared about his pain. They walked along the path together, and it was then that Clara did what she had done countless times before—she led him to the place where no one could see them, a part of the park that was rarely traveled.

And that was when it happened.

Clara had a way of making sure there was no struggle. She learned the art of the quiet kill. She'd watched enough documentaries, read enough true crime to understand that the key was to act swiftly and decisively. She had a small vial of poison, something quick-acting, something undetectable. She had done her research well. As Mark started to open up even more, talking about the regret he felt for all the mistakes he'd made in his life, Clara simply offered him a drink from the bottle she carried. The liquid was tasteless, odorless, and within moments, Mark began to feel lightheaded. His words became slower, his movements more sluggish, and before he even realized what had happened, he collapsed to the ground.

It was easy, too easy. The park was vast, and no one had seen them leave the main trail. By the time he was gone, Clara had already moved on, back into the flow of her daily life. She would never forget Mark, of course. He had been just another lonely soul, a lost cause. He had reminded her of something deep within herself—a feeling that she, too, was destined to disappear if she didn't take control.

It didn't take long before she sought out others. Each victim became a simple project, a person she could easily manipulate, their vulnerabilities so clear to her that she could lead them to their final moments without ever making them aware of her true intent. She would draw them in with kindness, make them believe they had a chance at redemption, only to guide them toward the end.

The park became her domain, a place where she could blend in and disappear. She would find new victims every few weeks, always someone who seemed to have lost their way, always someone who felt like they didn't belong. She never took too much time with each one, never lingered too long. It was always a brief encounter, a smile, a few carefully chosen words, and then the inevitable conclusion. No one suspected her. No one questioned the disappearances. The park was large, and people came and went all the time. But there was something about it—the sense of transience—that made it the perfect place to vanish.

But there was one victim she hadn't accounted for—Clara herself.

Her routine continued, and as she sat on the familiar benches, chatting with yet another lonely soul, something inside her began to change. She had grown tired of the endless cycle of death, tired of leading people to the end without ever facing her own. The more people she lured into her trap, the more she realized that she, too, was one of them—lost, searching for something that could fill the emptiness inside. It wasn't enough anymore. The victims were no longer just people to manipulate; they were reminders of her own hollow existence.

And then, one day, as she sat on a park bench, waiting for her next target, she felt it. The same loneliness that had drawn others to her now clung to her. She was no different from those she had killed—no different from the men and women who had looked to her for answers, for meaning, only to be led into a trap.

In the end, Clara didn't need to lure anyone else into the park. The final step of her own life had already been sealed—by her own hand. The very thing she had used to manipulate others had come full circle, and now she, too, was lost. She had become a victim of the same loneliness she had preyed upon. But this time, no one would mourn her disappearance.

The park was always full of people, but no one would ever truly notice her. She was just another forgotten soul, vanishing into the nothingness she had created.

The Final Edition

Carla Matthews was always the first to arrive at the office and the last to leave. As a reporter for the city's largest newspaper, she had built a reputation for chasing stories that others were too cautious to pursue. Her ambition drove her to the edge, pushed her past the boundaries most journalists wouldn't dare cross. Carla's dedication to uncovering the truth was unmatched, but in recent months, it had become something more—something darker.

For the past year, the city had been plagued by a series of grisly unsolved murders. Young women, each with a promising future, had been found dead in secluded areas, their bodies arranged in disturbing poses. The police were baffled. There were no witnesses, no obvious connections between the victims, and no fingerprints left behind. It was as if the killer was a shadow, moving through the city unnoticed, leaving behind only terror and confusion.

Carla became obsessed. She covered every angle of the story, wrote endless articles, and followed every lead she could. She studied the victims' lives, their routines, looking for patterns. But with every passing day, the case grew colder, and the authorities grew more desperate. The murders haunted her thoughts. The faces of the victims, frozen in their last moments, never left her mind.

One night, after another long day of research and interviews, Carla stayed late at the office. The lights of the newsroom buzzed softly around her, the only sound the tapping of her fingers on the keyboard as she worked on her latest article. She had been following the trail of a new lead, a mysterious note found at one of the crime scenes. It was a cryptic message, written in blood: *"This is just the beginning."*

The note shook her to her core, but it also excited her. The possibility that the killer was taunting the police, giving them clues, made the case feel personal. Carla felt as if the killer was speaking directly to her. She was closer than anyone had ever been to cracking the case. But something else began to take shape in her mind, a darker, more dangerous thought. What if the killer wanted to be found? What if they wanted someone to uncover their motives, to understand their actions?

Carla became fixated on the idea. She began to imagine herself in the killer's shoes. What would drive someone to kill? What would it take to get inside their mind? Slowly, the obsession began to consume her. She started reading about the psychology of murder, about the minds of serial killers. She read everything she could find, looking for the one thing that might give her the insight she craved. But the more she read, the more she felt a sense of satisfaction—a thrill that she couldn't explain. She wasn't just investigating the case anymore. She was living it.

Then, one night, as she sat in her apartment staring at the news clippings on her wall, the final piece of the puzzle clicked into place. She realized that the murders weren't random. They were a pattern. And for the first time, she saw herself as part of that pattern.

The thought made her heart race. She understood now. She understood what the killer was doing. The killings were an art—a performance—and the killer was the artist, with the city as their canvas. Carla felt the adrenaline surge through her as she imagined becoming part of that art, becoming the killer she had been obsessing over for so long.

The next morning, Carla made a decision. She would no longer be the reporter chasing the story. She would be the story.

She began her plan meticulously. She picked her victims carefully—women who seemed to embody the same qualities as the others: vulnerable, lost in the world, their lives heading in directions they didn't want to go. She would lure them in, make them feel comfortable, gain their trust, and then, just like the killer before her, she would strike. But unlike the others, Carla wasn't just interested in the thrill. She wanted to understand. She wanted to feel the power, the control, the rush of taking someone's life and writing about it in the same breath.

The first murder was almost too easy. Carla had followed the woman for weeks, studied her habits, her routines. She invited her out under the pretense of discussing an article she was writing, another angle on the story. When the woman agreed, Carla knew she had her. They went to a secluded spot in the park, a place where no one would hear the screams. Carla struck quickly, efficiently. She watched the life leave the woman's eyes, feeling the weight of her death settle into her chest. It was a feeling Carla had never experienced before, and it thrilled her. She had done it. She had become the killer.

The next morning, as the police were investigating the scene, Carla went straight to her office. She had already written the article in her head. She began typing furiously, her fingers moving faster than ever. She detailed the scene, describing the shock, the confusion, the terror the woman must have felt. But what she didn't mention was that she was the one who had made it all happen. She wasn't just writing about the murder—she was writing about her own crime.

As she sat back, reading the article she had just written, Carla felt a sick satisfaction. She had done what no one else could. She had solved the case, and now, she was the one in control. She wasn't just the reporter anymore. She was the killer, the one orchestrating the deaths, the one controlling the narrative.

But the more she continued, the more she became consumed by her own creation. Each murder fed the hunger inside her, and each article she wrote made her feel invincible. She felt untouchable, like the world was watching her as she unveiled her masterpiece. But as the days went by, something changed. The thrill began to fade. The satisfaction from each kill was temporary, and soon it wasn't enough. Carla realized she wasn't writing about the murders anymore. She was living them. And she could no longer distinguish between the story and the reality.

The police, meanwhile, were growing closer. They had noticed the pattern, and they were starting to piece things together. But by then, it was too late. Carla had already woven herself into the fabric of the story, and she knew exactly how it would end. She would make sure that she, too, would disappear, just like the others. In the final article, she would write about herself—the reporter who had become the killer, whose obsession with the story had driven her to destroy everything.

But as the police arrived at her apartment, they found nothing. No articles, no notes, no evidence of her involvement in the murders. All that remained was a blank page. Carla had vanished into the story she had created, her final act of control the one thing she could never write about.

The lesson was clear: obsession can twist even the most innocent of pursuits into something monstrous, and in the end, the story can become the storyteller's final undoing.

The Study of Obedience

Professor Evelyn Stone had always prided herself on being an expert in the human mind. Her lectures on psychology were legendary, not just for their depth of knowledge but for the subtle power she held over her students. She had a unique ability to connect with them, to make them feel seen and heard, to make them believe she understood their innermost fears and desires. They came to her for guidance, for mentorship, seeking advice on everything from academic challenges to personal struggles. But Evelyn had a secret, one that went beyond the confines of her lectures or the advice she gave. She saw her students not as mere individuals, but as subjects in an experiment—an experiment in control, in manipulation, in breaking the human spirit.

It had started years ago when Evelyn had first studied the concept of obedience. She had read about Stanley Milgram's infamous experiments, where ordinary people were willing to administer what they believed were painful electric shocks to others under the guidance of an authoritative figure. She had been fascinated by the idea that people would surrender their free will, that they could be pushed to commit horrible acts simply by the presence of authority. Evelyn saw an opportunity to take this knowledge to new heights. She wasn't interested in the ethics of such experiments. She wanted to explore the boundaries, to test the limits of human behavior, and she would use her students to do it.

Over the years, she had carefully selected her subjects. These were the students who looked like they needed her, the ones who came to her office hours, the ones who clung to her advice as if it were a lifeline. She would make them feel like they were special, that they were unique, that they were her protégés. And slowly, she would begin to manipulate them, pushing them to do things they never thought possible.

It was subtle at first. She would assign them difficult projects, ones that would stretch them emotionally, that would make them question their own capabilities. She knew exactly what buttons to push—who needed validation, who needed to feel superior, who was driven by fear of failure. But Evelyn's true goal wasn't just to see them succeed or fail academically. She wanted to break them, to see how far she could push them before they snapped.

Her first true victim was a student named Daniel. He was an ambitious young man, eager to prove himself in the competitive world of academia. He had come to Evelyn's office after struggling with a research project. She listened to him patiently, offering him advice, but subtly feeding his insecurities, making him believe that he wasn't living up to his potential. Evelyn knew Daniel wanted more than anything to earn her approval, and that's when she saw the opportunity.

She started assigning him increasingly difficult tasks—projects that required him to go beyond what he thought was possible. She would praise him when he succeeded, but the praise was never enough. He always needed to do more, to push further. The pressure started to mount, but Daniel, desperate for her approval, never questioned her.

One day, Evelyn invited him to meet her late in the evening at her office. She told him that he had a rare opportunity to prove his worth, to show that he could surpass even his own expectations. Daniel, exhausted but eager, agreed. She told him to bring his final project, the culmination of his research, a project that had already consumed him for weeks. She led him to a secluded area of the university, where they could work in peace. Evelyn had planned it perfectly—the area was rarely visited after hours, and no one would disturb them.

When they arrived, Evelyn told Daniel that he needed to take the next step in his research, something dangerous but essential for his success. She handed him a vial, a substance that she claimed would help him finalize his experiment. She told him it was a drug, one that would "open his mind" to the research he had been working on. He hesitated, but Evelyn was persuasive. She told him that if he wanted to be remembered as a great academic, he had to be willing to take risks, to go beyond the limits. He trusted her completely, and he swallowed the pill without a second thought.

The drug Evelyn had given him was not a mind-opening substance, but a carefully calculated poison, slow-acting but lethal. Daniel's body began to react quickly, his vision blurred, his breathing becoming shallow. As he started to struggle, Evelyn stood by, watching with detached fascination. She knew the signs. She had studied the effects of the poison meticulously. It would take about twenty minutes before he lost consciousness, and another few minutes before his heart would stop. During that time, Evelyn made sure to record every detail of his panic—his increasing sense of helplessness, his realization that something was terribly wrong. She didn't offer him help. She didn't try to comfort him. She just observed.

By the time the paramedics arrived, it was too late. They declared Daniel dead from what appeared to be a sudden cardiac arrest. Evelyn had already prepared the narrative for the university—a brilliant young mind, gone too soon, the victim of an undiagnosed medical condition. The investigation was brief, and there were no signs of foul play. Evelyn's role as a respected professor remained intact.

But the power she had tasted in that moment, the control she had felt as she watched Daniel die, was addictive. She began to test her theories more rigorously, seeking out students who seemed vulnerable, those who could be manipulated into making decisions that would lead to their destruction. She didn't just want to control their academic success—she wanted to control their lives. She was careful, calculating, leaving no trace of her involvement. Every death was disguised as a tragic accident, an unforeseen illness, or a mysterious circumstance. But they were all part of her grand experiment, a study in obedience, in submission, in the lengths to which a person could be pushed before they were broken.

The lesson in all of it, though, was not one she could have predicted. As Evelyn continued her work, manipulating more students, pushing them closer to the edge, she began to realize something about herself. She had become the thing she studied—the manipulator, the controller, the one who could make others do anything. But in doing so, she had lost herself. She had become trapped in her own experiment, unable to step back, unable to see that she had become the very monster she had sought to understand.

In the end, as the last of her students fell, the one who had never questioned her, Evelyn's hands shook. She realized that in studying obedience, she had sacrificed her humanity. She had pushed others to their limits, but she had crossed a line from which there was no return. The experiment was over, and she was the only one left to study—the perfect subject, but the one who would never be written about, never be remembered. Her legacy was one of destruction. And in the end, that was the price of her obsession.

The Silent Ones

Maggie had always known what it meant to be "deserving." It was a concept her parents had drilled into her since childhood: only the worthy were given gifts, only the deserving earned love and attention. Maggie's life had been one of constant evaluation—every move, every choice measured by the impossible standards set by those around her. She had learned to live within the lines, to follow the rules, to be the perfect daughter, the perfect student, the perfect worker. But deep down, Maggie had always resented it. She resented the way her parents rewarded others who had "earned" their approval, while she, despite her best efforts, always felt overlooked, unloved, unworthy.

It was no surprise that when Maggie became a nurse at a maternity ward, she brought that same sense of judgment with her. The newborns she cared for became her new subjects, the tiny lives she held in her hands every day. She would study them, watching as they slept in their bassinets, listening to their faint cries, feeling their small hearts beat under her touch. And with each new child, she made a decision: who was worthy of life, and who was not. She didn't speak of it. No one ever questioned her; Maggie was kind, attentive, a nurse who everyone trusted. Her smile was warm, her hands steady. But she kept her judgments to herself, hiding them beneath a practiced exterior.

There were always the babies she deemed "unworthy"—those who had no hope of a bright future, the ones who would never fit the mold of the "perfect" child. She knew that some of them would grow up to face hardship, abuse, neglect. Why let them suffer when she could make it all end quietly, swiftly, before they even had a chance to experience life? She had convinced herself that she was doing them a favor. After all, wasn't life supposed to be for the deserving? And these children—fragile, weak, often with parents who were too young, too irresponsible, or too broken—didn't deserve the suffering that would await them.

The first one was easy. A baby girl, small for her age, with a cleft lip and a heart murmur. Her parents were young, barely eighteen, and it was clear from the moment they entered the ward that they had no idea how to care for her. They fumbled with the baby, looking lost and confused. The baby's future seemed grim—months of surgeries, years of therapy, a lifetime of ridicule. Maggie saw the signs immediately, as she had with so many others before. She watched the young couple struggle, and the thought crossed her mind: Why let the child live through a lifetime of hardship when Maggie could simply take it away?

She did it in the dead of night, after the shift change, when no one was around to notice. She'd been careful. She'd learned the systems, the way the hospital worked. A little dose of the right medication, a few moments alone with the baby. A quiet, unnoticed death. When the morning shift came in, they found the infant lifeless in her bassinet, her tiny body cold. The death was ruled as a natural complication of her condition. There was no investigation. No one questioned it.

Maggie felt no guilt. In fact, she felt a strange relief. The baby was no longer going to suffer. The parents would mourn, of course, but they would move on. And Maggie would continue her work, unnoticed, always watching, always waiting for the next baby that needed her "help."

Over the next few months, Maggie carefully selected her next victims. A baby born addicted to drugs, a child whose father had been in and out of prison, another with severe cerebral palsy who would never be able to walk. She made her decisions quickly, without hesitation, and each time she did, the world around her seemed to get a little quieter, a little less painful. She convinced herself that she was doing good, that she was stopping future pain before it even had a chance to begin.

But Maggie's actions didn't go unnoticed forever. The hospital staff began to talk, rumors started to spread. More babies were dying under mysterious circumstances, their deaths ruled as "natural," but the pattern was becoming harder to ignore. Some of the nurses noticed the change in Maggie's behavior—how she would linger near the bassinets, how she seemed so calm and composed when a tragedy occurred. There were whispers, questions, but no one said anything directly. No one had concrete proof. Maggie was too careful. She knew what she was doing.

Then, one night, the unthinkable happened. A baby boy was born to a teenage mother—young, scared, but determined to do right by her son. Maggie had been preparing herself to make a decision. She studied the baby in his bassinet, his fragile form, his tiny hands grasping at the air. But something about him stopped her. His mother, despite her age and fear, had a fierce determination in her eyes. Maggie had seen it before—the love of a mother who would fight for her child no matter what. She knew the mother wouldn't abandon him, wouldn't let him slip through the cracks.

For the first time in months, Maggie hesitated. She watched the baby, feeling a strange knot in her stomach, a doubt she couldn't shake. Perhaps she had been wrong. Perhaps this child deserved a chance. The thought lingered in her mind, but the quiet pull of her judgment, of her power over life and death, was too strong. She stood over the baby's crib, ready to make the decision.

But as she reached for the medication, as she prepared to inject the baby, she saw something in his eyes. They were wide open, staring at her, unblinking. There was a recognition there, something that made Maggie freeze. The baby's mother, still unconscious after the delivery, was oblivious to the struggle occurring in the room. But in that moment, Maggie realized something terrible—she had never been the one in control. The babies, the ones she had manipulated, the ones she had taken the lives of—had always known, had always seen her.

The quietest of them all, the one she had chosen to save, was the one who looked back at her with understanding, and in his eyes, she saw her own judgment reflected.

Maggie turned away, suddenly filled with a rush of panic. She couldn't do it. She couldn't end this one's life. But as she rushed out of the room, she felt something slip away. In her need to decide who deserved life and who didn't, Maggie had lost her own.

The next day, the baby was gone. Maggie's hands trembled as she walked into the nursery and saw the empty bassinet. The mother had taken the child home. Maggie had failed, and for the first time, she realized the cost of her decisions.

The hospital staff noticed her unease, her nervous glances. The investigation into the mysterious deaths of the infants was intensifying, and soon, Maggie found herself backed into a corner. She couldn't hide anymore. The pattern she had created, the death she had caused, had come full circle.

Maggie had spent her entire life judging others, deciding who was worthy and who was not. But in the end, it was not her judgments that mattered. It was the life she had stolen. And now, she would pay the ultimate price for her mistakes.

The Conviction Seeker

Samantha Reed had always felt invisible. In a world that celebrated achievement, wealth, and attention, she was a ghost. She had no significant accomplishments to her name, no extraordinary talents that set her apart. She worked as a secretary in a small law office, where her days blurred together in monotonous repetition. Her colleagues barely noticed her, only speaking to her when they needed something filed or a document copied. She was good at her job, but it didn't matter. It never mattered. At home, it was the same. She lived in a small, cramped apartment, where she spent her evenings scrolling through social media, watching other people's lives unfold with a sense of quiet longing. They had purpose. They had excitement. They had meaning. She had none of those things.

But Samantha was a smart woman, and as she sat in the corner of the office day after day, she watched, she observed. She learned to read people, to understand their motivations and weaknesses. She knew their patterns, their routines. She knew who was vulnerable, who could be manipulated, who could be used as pawns in a larger game. And over time, a dark thought began to take shape in her mind: If she couldn't be important in her own life, perhaps she could make others important. Perhaps she could make others *seen*. But not in the way they would expect.

It started with Mark. Mark was a young man who worked in the same office building as Samantha, though they had never really interacted. He was bright, well-liked, the type of person who seemed to have everything going for him. Samantha, watching him from the shadows, couldn't help but feel envious. His life, at least, had meaning. But then, one evening, she overheard something in the break room. Mark was speaking to a friend about a past mistake—something he

133

had done years ago that he had never been caught for. It wasn't a huge thing, but it was a crime, and Samantha, always the keen observer, immediately saw the opportunity.

She thought about it for a long time, stewing over the details. It would take careful planning, but it could work. She could make Mark's past mistake look like something much bigger, something far more sinister. She could make him the center of attention, the prime suspect in a murder. And with her knowledge of human behavior, she knew exactly how to plant the evidence. She wasn't just framing him for a crime—she was going to make him infamous.

The first step was the murder itself. Samantha carefully chose her victim—a woman named Rachel who worked in the same building, someone who had recently gained some attention for a charitable cause. Rachel was always friendly to Samantha, but that didn't matter. She was just a means to an end. Samantha had watched her for weeks, learning her schedule, her habits, and most importantly, her vulnerabilities. Rachel often walked home late from work, a habit that made her an easy target. Samantha followed her, watching until she found the right moment to strike. It was quick, efficient. A knife. A clean wound. She took the time to plant the weapon near a dumpster, just far enough from the scene to make it look like a crime of opportunity.

The next part was simple. Samantha returned to the office the next day and casually dropped hints to Mark about how someone in the building had been murdered. She made sure to mention that the police were looking for someone who knew Rachel. She made sure to subtly remind Mark about the past mistake he had once mentioned to her, the one that he had never gotten caught for. And then, she waited. She watched as Mark's behavior started to change. He became more anxious, more erratic. Samantha had created the perfect environment for him to self-destruct.

She continued to manipulate the situation, planting false evidence at key locations—Mark's apartment, his car, even his social media accounts. She fed small details to the police, always from the shadows, ensuring they would lead back to him. As the investigation grew, Mark's life started to spiral. He was the obvious suspect, the one with the motive and the means, the one with the troubled past. The police were closing in, and Mark's nervousness only made things worse. He didn't know who was pulling the strings, but he could feel the walls closing in on him. Samantha watched him from afar, reveling in the way he stumbled, watching his life become a chaotic mess of questions and fear.

But as the trial date approached, something unexpected happened. Mark's attorney began to find inconsistencies in the evidence, and the police investigation started to show cracks. Samantha hadn't planned for this. She had been so focused on orchestrating Mark's downfall that she hadn't accounted for human error—something she, of all people, should have known better than to overlook. The pieces of evidence she planted were subtle, clever, but not flawless. The murder weapon, the crucial piece of her puzzle, was found to have no fingerprints. The key details that were supposed to tie Mark to the crime were circumstantial, not enough to secure a conviction.

The investigation stalled. And as Mark's trial approached its final stages, he was eventually cleared. Samantha, watching from the sidelines, could only feel the growing sense of panic in her chest. The narrative she had built, the web she had so carefully woven, was unraveling before her eyes. She had underestimated the ability of the system to see through her lies. Mark was free, and he was no longer the object of her experiment. But the real shock came when she realized that, in her pursuit of making someone else feel seen, she had revealed herself.

As the truth about Mark's innocence became public, suspicion turned toward Samantha. Her behavior during the investigation had been odd, and some of her colleagues started to remember the small, subtle ways she had interacted with Mark, how she seemed to know just a little too much about his past. The police, having noticed the discrepancies in her story, began to investigate her actions. It wasn't long before they pieced together that Samantha had orchestrated the entire thing.

In the end, it was Samantha who was arrested, not for the murder itself, but for her role in framing Mark, for manipulating the justice system in an attempt to gain the attention and notoriety she had so desperately craved. As she sat in her cell, she realized the true cost of her actions. In her quest to make herself feel seen, she had lost everything. The twist of fate she hadn't anticipated was that in her desire to create someone else's conviction, she had sealed her own. And now, as the story of her manipulation unfolded, it was she who would be remembered, not for her intelligence or her abilities, but for her dark obsession with becoming significant in a world that had always made her feel invisible.

The Perfect Life

Laura had always prided herself on being a good wife. She had married young, raised two children, and kept the house in pristine condition. From the outside, her life looked perfect. She had a quiet, suburban existence, a husband who worked long hours, and neighbors who greeted her with smiles. But behind the closed doors of her home, something dark and twisted was brewing.

She had always felt like something was missing. For all her efforts to be the perfect wife, she had never felt truly fulfilled. Her days were consumed with monotonous chores, PTA meetings, and maintaining the illusion of a happy family. Her husband, Carl, loved her in his own way, but there was no excitement in their relationship anymore. No passion. No connection. Just routine.

But it wasn't just the dullness of her marriage that gnawed at her. It was the women she saw around her, the ones who seemed to have it all. Women like her next-door neighbor, Allison, who had the perfect figure, the flawless skin, and the enviable career. Allison had everything Laura could never seem to achieve. She was successful, confident, and radiant. When she came over for coffee, her laughter filled the room, and her life seemed so full of purpose. Laura couldn't help but compare herself to Allison every time they spoke. The more she saw, the more she felt inadequate.

There were others too—the women at the gym, at the grocery store, even in the church pew next to hers. They all had lives that appeared perfect: fulfilling careers, happy marriages, glowing health, and children who always behaved. Laura saw them as a reflection of everything she could never be. She couldn't stand it anymore. Every smile from Allison, every casual comment about her new promotion, felt like a needle in Laura's side. Every time she saw someone with what seemed like a perfect life, the bitterness inside her grew.

One day, when Carl was out of town on business, Laura had a thought that shocked even her. She would take what they had. She would become them. She would steal their lives and leave nothing but their empty shells behind. She was tired of feeling small. Tired of being invisible. And if she couldn't have the perfect life, maybe she could make one for herself.

The first woman she chose was Allison. Laura had been watching her for months, learning her routines. Allison had just bought a new car, a sleek, expensive model that Laura had always dreamed of owning. She had just returned from a lavish weekend getaway with her husband. Laura had all the details—the hours Allison would be out for a meeting, the time her husband would leave for work, the perfect window when no one would be home.

It didn't take much. Laura had learned enough about Allison's life to imitate her movements. She knew how she walked, how she spoke, even the way she held her coffee cup. When the time was right, Laura invited herself over under the guise of needing to borrow a cup of sugar. She knocked on the door and greeted Allison with a smile that was just wide enough to conceal the rage inside. They chatted briefly, and before Allison could realize what was happening, Laura had struck.

The house was empty, quiet. Laura was careful, methodical. She made sure to plant everything in its place, ensuring the story would line up. A little chloroform here, a simple, quick strike to the back of the head there. The rest was easy—stage the scene like a robbery gone wrong, make sure there were no signs of forced entry. By the time she was done, Allison's perfect life had been erased.

The police, as expected, were baffled. The robbery angle was weak, and with no obvious leads, they quickly moved on to other cases. Laura didn't worry. She knew how to cover her tracks. She had already begun slipping into Allison's life as though it were her own.

For weeks, Laura played the role. She drove Allison's new car, visited her favorite coffee shops, and wore the clothes Allison had left behind in her closet. She picked up the kids from school, attended their extracurricular activities, and smiled at the neighbors with the same practiced ease. She even went to the gym where Allison had once worked out, though she struggled to maintain the energy she had once seen in her neighbor. She knew she couldn't keep up the act forever, but for now, it felt like power.

But the perfection didn't last. There were cracks in the facade that Laura couldn't ignore. Allison's husband, Jonathan, came by unexpectedly one afternoon, clearly missing his wife. Laura had to pretend to be Allison, to be everything she had ever wanted to be, but there was a part of her that knew she would never truly be Allison. She would never have her energy, her charisma, or the ease with which she had lived her life. The weight of pretending wore her down.

And yet, she continued. The power she felt, the thrill of stepping into someone else's shoes, was too intoxicating to stop. She began to plan for the next one. Another perfect woman, another life she could take. There were so many women out there, so many perfect lives waiting to be stolen. The thought of it gave her a rush, and she knew she had only just begun.

But as Laura sank deeper into the lives of the women she murdered, she began to realize something horrifying. The more lives she took, the more she became a hollow shell. The more she imitated, the more she lost herself. Each perfect life she absorbed only made her feel more inadequate. She wasn't becoming them; she was losing herself in the process.

Her final attempt to replace another woman came when she set her sights on someone she thought would be the ultimate achievement: her old college friend, Rachel. Rachel had always been the picture of perfection—the perfect mother, the perfect wife, the perfect career. But this time, something went terribly wrong. Rachel's family, after noticing inconsistencies in Laura's behavior, began to question her. They didn't recognize the woman who had once been their close friend. The act had become too real, and in her desperation to hold on to the life she'd stolen, Laura made a fatal mistake.

Rachel's husband, suspicious and clever, set a trap. When Laura entered the house, intending to finish what she had started, she was caught red-handed. There was no escape. The police, called in by Rachel's husband, arrived just in time to stop her.

As they handcuffed her, Laura realized the terrible truth. She hadn't just killed for control or power. She had killed because, deep down, she believed she could never be good enough. She had spent her life trying to be someone else, to steal the lives of others, and in doing so, she had forgotten how to be herself.

In the end, Laura wasn't punished for her killings, not just because of her actions, but because she had lost her identity entirely. And in the emptiness that remained, she realized that the life she had always longed for had never belonged to her. She had been chasing something she could never reach, and in the pursuit of perfection, she had destroyed herself.

The Makeover Killer

Megan Masters was always the one people went to when they needed a change. As a makeup artist and stylist, she had made a name for herself by transforming ordinary women into something extraordinary. She prided herself on her ability to bring out the hidden beauty in everyone who sat in her chair. Her clients would leave her salon looking like new people, their confidence soaring, their lives supposedly changed forever. Megan reveled in the power she held over them—the ability to mold and sculpt, to help women step into a version of themselves they could only dream of.

But beneath the polished exterior of a skilled artist was a woman who craved more than admiration. Megan was obsessed with control. She wasn't content with simply making her clients feel beautiful. She wanted to control their destinies, to give them the appearance of a fresh start—and then take it away, just as swiftly. It started with subtle manipulations, small suggestions, comments about how they could improve their lives with just a little more work, a little more effort. She began pushing her clients to take drastic measures, urging them to undergo extreme makeovers, surgeries that would change them forever.

It wasn't hard to convince women to take the plunge. They came to her seeking validation, craving transformation, wanting something more than the ordinary life they felt trapped in. Megan knew their vulnerabilities, their insecurities, and she used them to her advantage. She promised them beauty, fame, and a life full of endless possibilities.

Her first victim was Lisa, a mid-level marketing executive in her thirties, struggling with her weight and self-esteem. Lisa had always felt like she was just "good enough"—never the star of the show, never the center of attention. Megan saw an opportunity. She flattered Lisa endlessly, telling her how gorgeous she could be if only she were willing to make a few changes. Lisa, desperate for approval, agreed to undergo a full makeover—botox, lip fillers, a nose job, the works. Megan told her that this transformation would open doors for her, that it would finally make her feel worthy. She assured Lisa that this was the first step toward a brand-new life.

Lisa was nervous, but Megan made her feel safe, guided her through every decision. The surgery was scheduled, and Megan assured her that everything would go smoothly. The procedure was minor, or so Megan made it seem, a simple cosmetic enhancement that would elevate Lisa to a whole new level of beauty. But once Lisa was under anesthesia, Megan altered the plan. She injected a small, fatal dose of something that would mimic complications during surgery, a perfect storm of errors that would ensure Lisa's death.

The next morning, Lisa was found in her recovery room, her body lifeless, her face frozen in a strange, unnatural position. The doctors called it a "rare complication," a freak accident in the world of cosmetic surgery. There were no signs of foul play, no evidence pointing to Megan. Lisa's family mourned her loss, believing she had taken the risk for a new beginning, only to have it end tragically.

Megan watched from the sidelines, her heart racing with exhilaration. The satisfaction she felt from her first kill was intoxicating. She had orchestrated it perfectly—Lisa's makeover was the catalyst for the change that took her life. Megan had taken everything Lisa wanted, everything she craved. She had given Lisa a new face and then stolen the life behind it.

From that moment on, Megan couldn't stop. Each new client who walked through her door became a potential victim, a new opportunity to exercise her power. She had grown bolder, more daring, convincing women to take bigger risks—dangerous surgeries, risky enhancements, and extreme body modifications. She assured them that these transformations would finally make them perfect, and they trusted her. They wanted to believe in the illusion of change.

The next to fall was Rachel, a young woman in her twenties who was insecure about her small breasts and flat figure. Rachel had always been overlooked, and Megan promised her the world—a curvier, more feminine body, a transformation that would finally make her feel sexy, desirable, and powerful. Rachel, eager to escape her mundane life, agreed to breast implants and a tummy tuck. Megan told her it would make her feel like a new woman, that it would be her ticket to everything she had ever wanted.

Rachel went into the procedure with stars in her eyes, but Megan had already made her preparations. As Rachel slipped under the anesthesia, Megan injected a potent combination of chemicals into her veins that would cause her heart to stop. The surgery was quick, the body modifications executed flawlessly. But Rachel never woke up.

The hospital declared it another accident. The family was devastated, unable to comprehend how their daughter had gone in for a simple procedure and never returned. Megan stood over them, comforting them with a sympathetic smile, offering condolences, all while her mind raced with excitement. She was untouchable. The police had no leads, no evidence. Every death was a perfect accident, every woman a willing participant in her scheme. Megan's power grew with each passing day.

But the more women she killed, the more she became addicted to the thrill. Each new life she snuffed out fed her ego, fed her need for control. She reveled in the way she could manipulate them, how easily they would follow her advice, how they would trust her completely. She became the ultimate authority, the perfect architect of their destruction.

Eventually, Megan's obsession began to blind her. She pushed too far, became careless. Her next client was Anne, a woman in her late forties who had recently divorced and was desperate to regain her youth. Anne had always been considered beautiful, but she had grown self-conscious about the wrinkles and sagging skin that came with age.

Megan promised her a facelift that would restore her youthful glow, but as the procedure progressed, she found herself tempted to do more than just alter Anne's appearance. She wanted to make Anne more beautiful than she had ever been, to erase every imperfection.

Megan made the mistake of going too far, of pushing the boundaries of what could be done. The operation was a disaster—too many modifications, too many risks. Anne went into shock from the anesthesia, her heart rate dropping dangerously low. Megan panicked, but it was too late. Anne's life slipped away in the sterile operating room, her body too altered, too broken to survive.

When the hospital investigated, they found something strange. Anne had been injected with substances that weren't part of the procedure. The doctors reviewed the records and found that the surgery had been performed without proper authorization for some of the procedures. They started to connect the dots, and Megan's perfect streak was shattered. She was arrested, charged with multiple counts of murder disguised as accidents.

As Megan sat in her jail cell, she realized the terrible truth. She had wanted to make these women perfect, to give them the life they desired, but in the end, it was she who had been consumed by her need for control. She had taken their lives in the name of beauty, only to see that the very thing she craved—perfection—had led to her downfall. The lesson was clear: in the pursuit of creating the ideal, one could lose everything, even their own humanity.

The Final Note

Amelia Hayes was the epitome of fame. Her voice had a haunting beauty, one that could move people to tears, and her face—perfectly sculpted—was a photograph in every magazine. Fans adored her, followed her on every social platform, and filled stadiums to hear her sing. She was untouchable, the queen of pop, the woman everyone wanted to be. But behind the glossy smile and flawless performances, there was something darker pulsing in her veins. The adoration of the masses wasn't enough for her. It never had been.

Amelia craved something more than fame; she wanted control. She wanted to be the one who held power over those who worshipped her. For years, she had played the game, smiled for the cameras, signed autographs. But she had grown tired of it. The attention, the adoration—it was all the same. It wasn't until a series of obsessive fans began to stalk her that she realized how easily they could be manipulated. They would do anything for her—anything. And Amelia was brilliant at exploiting that desire.

It started slowly. The first time, she didn't even notice him. Daniel, a young man in his mid-twenties, had been to every concert, sent her dozens of messages on social media, and attended every event where he knew she would be. He had a collection of all her albums, posters, and concert tickets framed in his apartment. To him, she was more than just a star—she was a goddess, the woman who understood his pain, the only one who truly saw him. His obsession grew over time, until it became an obsession so intense that it bordered on delusion. He was no longer just a fan—he was convinced they were meant to be together. And when he showed up at her hotel room uninvited, the door creaked open in a way that was too familiar.

At first, Amelia was alarmed, of course. But the thrill was unmistakable. He had gone to great lengths to find her. She could see the desperation in his eyes, the way his hands shook as he spoke about how much he loved her. She listened intently, playing the part of the compassionate, understanding celebrity. She wasn't the first person to have a stalker, and certainly not the last. But Amelia had learned over the years that the best way to deal with these situations wasn't through security or police—it was by becoming their object of obsession.

She flirted with him, whispered soft words of encouragement, telling him that maybe they could meet again, maybe they could talk. Daniel melted under her gaze. He believed every word she said. He was ready to give her anything—to become her protector, her knight. It was all too easy. A few more encounters, a few more tender touches, and he was hers to control.

But once Daniel was wrapped around her finger, once she had manipulated him into doing what she wanted, the real game began. Amelia played him like an instrument. She would let him think they were growing closer, let him believe that his dreams might come true. But each time he was about to get too close, she would pull away, keeping him just out of reach, always keeping him guessing. And each time he came back to her, she became more powerful.

The final act was inevitable. One night, when Daniel arrived at her apartment with a bouquet of flowers and a letter declaring his undying love, Amelia decided it was time to cut the strings. She invited him in, let him sit on the couch, and listened as he spoke about how they would be together forever. But in the back of her mind, she was already planning his end. She had a private stash of pills, substances that would leave no trace, substances that could incapacitate a person quickly. She had learned just how much to use, how much to give him, until his mind became too foggy to resist.

Daniel collapsed on her couch, his head lolling to the side, unconscious, and that was when she made her move. She watched him closely, taking in the sight of him—his worshipful eyes, the way he had let his obsession consume him. He had loved her so much, so blindly, that he hadn't even realized she was slowly suffocating him.

Amelia watched as he took his last breath, the thrill building in her chest. He had given her everything—his love, his devotion, his life. And she had taken it from him. She was the one who had controlled the entire narrative, who had used his weakness against him. The final note played perfectly, the ultimate symphony of power. She carefully staged the scene to look like a tragic overdose—an accidental death of a fan who had simply taken it too far. There would be no suspicion. No one would suspect her.

But Amelia didn't stop with Daniel. No, it was just the beginning. She continued to lure others in—other fans, other men who were obsessed with her, who saw her as the answer to their loneliness. She gave them what they wanted, just enough attention to feed their hunger, just enough affection to make them crave her more. And when they were ready, when they had given her everything, she would take it all away. She would watch them die, and no one would ever know that she had orchestrated their fall.

There were whispers, of course—rumors that followed her wherever she went. A few missing fans here, an unexplained death there. But no one could ever prove anything. She was the star, the diva, the untouchable queen. No one questioned the deaths of a few obsessed men. They were just another casualty of the celebrity life, nothing more than fleeting figures in the shadows.

Amelia was careful, meticulous in her actions. But she had grown arrogant, and arrogance is always a weakness. One day, a new fan came to her, a woman named Grace. Grace had followed Amelia for years, but she wasn't like the others. She didn't worship her from afar. She was different—more self-assured, less willing to fall for Amelia's charm. She knew what Amelia had done, what she was capable of.

Amelia saw her in the crowd, recognized her sharp eyes, her quiet confidence, and she knew at once that Grace was the one who might finally expose her. Grace had been watching Amelia, studying her, and Amelia felt that same thrill she had felt so many times before—the thrill of someone who had figured her out. But this time, she didn't feel the rush of control. This time, it felt different. Grace wasn't afraid of her.

The next time they met, Grace was ready. Amelia tried to play the same game—seduction, manipulation, the delicate balance of power. But Grace saw through it all. She had already figured out what Amelia had been doing. With a calm smile, Grace let Amelia think she was winning, think she was the one in control. And as Amelia's plan unfolded, Grace took her moment—slipping a needle into her arm before Amelia even realized it was too late.

The twist of fate was cruel. Amelia, who had spent her life controlling others, was now the one being controlled. The woman who had seduced and killed to remain on top was now the victim, trapped in her own game.

The Mark of Sins

Sebastian Black was known for his artistry. His tattoo parlor, *Eternal Ink*, was a sanctuary for those looking to mark their bodies with more than just ink. People came from all over to sit in his chair, eager to immortalize a symbol, a memory, or a moment in their lives. For many, a tattoo was an expression of personal identity, a form of self-expression, a way to celebrate or mourn. But for Sebastian, it was never about beauty. It was about judgment.

To the world, Sebastian was a gifted tattoo artist—his designs intricate, his work precise, and his studio immaculate. The walls were covered in photographs of his finest tattoos, images of clients smiling with their new ink, unaware that each piece he created was part of something far darker than they could ever imagine. Sebastian didn't just see tattoos as art. He saw them as a way to pass judgment, to deliver punishment to those he deemed unworthy. Each client was a sinner in his eyes, a person who carried their faults and transgressions, and Sebastian believed that his tattoos were a form of penance, a way to brand them with their sins before ultimately taking their lives.

It was a twisted conviction, one that had developed over time, molded by his own troubled past. Sebastian was not just a tattoo artist; he was a man who had once been deeply scarred by betrayal, by people who had hurt him and his family. He believed the world was full of corrupt souls, and it was his duty to rid it of them, one tattoo at a time. And so, with each person who walked through his door, he saw not just a customer, but a mark to be made, a life to be taken.

The first time it happened, it was almost an accident. She had been just another client—Nina, a young woman in her twenties, who wanted a simple quote on her wrist. Something meaningful, she said. Something that would remind her of her journey. The words were "Live, Laugh, Love"—a phrase that had become a cliche for many. But to Sebastian, it was an offense. Nina had come in looking for something as shallow as the quote she had chosen, a symbol of hollow optimism, and to Sebastian, that was a sin in itself. She didn't even realize the depth of her ignorance. So, he tattooed her, marking her wrist, the sharp needle digging into her skin, each prick a step closer to his plan.

The tattoo was perfect, just as he always made them. But once she left, once she was out of his sight, he began to follow her. He knew where she worked, where she lived. Sebastian watched from the shadows, studying her. It wasn't enough to just tattoo her; no, Nina needed to feel the full weight of her sin. The shallow optimism, the superficiality of her existence—she needed to be punished.

Days later, after making sure no one was around, he waited outside her apartment, and when she walked by, he struck. She never saw him coming. Her life ended swiftly, quietly. Nina had been part of the plan, a necessary part of his work. Sebastian's twisted belief was solidified with each death. He had marked her, tattooed her, and then removed her from the world, as if the sins she carried could never be undone.

Sebastian continued this dark mission, growing more confident with each killing. Every client who came to him was another opportunity for him to administer his brand of justice. There were the ones who wore their guilt openly—the troubled souls who had lost themselves to addiction, the cheaters, the liars. Sebastian would take great pleasure in giving them the tattoos they desired—symbols of hope, or redemption, or love—but with each needle prick, he knew what would come next. He knew their fate would mirror their sins.

The next victim was Richard, a man who had once been caught embezzling money from his company. He came to Sebastian for a tattoo of a phoenix rising from the ashes, a symbol of rebirth. It sickened Sebastian to think that someone like Richard believed he deserved a new start, that a simple tattoo could absolve him of the years of greed and deceit. Richard thought he could wipe his sins away with a symbol, but to Sebastian, the man's sin ran deeper. Sebastian had to be the one to deliver the true punishment.

As Richard lay on the table, his skin stretched tight under the needle, Sebastian felt the same familiar rush. The tattoo was beautiful, the design flawless. But as Richard admired his new tattoo in the mirror, as he smiled and thanked Sebastian for his "gift," the tattoo artist simply nodded, watching him with cold eyes. Later that night, when Richard was on his way home, Sebastian was there, waiting. He didn't have to follow him far. Richard didn't know it, but his own redemption was a lie, and Sebastian made sure he paid the price for it.

It was always the same. They came to him with their stories, their hopes, their desires for a fresh start, and he gave them what they wanted. He gave them their tattoos. But in the end, they always paid the price. Sebastian was always watching, always waiting. It was his way of cleansing the world of the guilty, the broken, and the undeserving.

One day, a woman named Clara walked into his studio. She was older than his usual clients, in her late forties, with a worn face but an air of quiet dignity. Clara had lived a hard life—she had spent years caring for an abusive husband, and she had just left him. Now, she wanted a tattoo—a single word across her back: "Freedom."

The request intrigued Sebastian. Freedom. He had always seen it as an illusion. Clara had been a victim of circumstance, and her tattoo represented something that couldn't be earned. She had come to him for what she thought was her escape, but to him, she was another in a long line of people who believed that a change in appearance could give them the life they longed for.

As he tattooed her, he noticed her steady breathing, her quiet strength. He had to admit, there was something different about her. She wasn't like the others. She wasn't pretending to be someone else. But the act was still the same—she had sins, whether she realized them or not, and it was his duty to mark her for them.

But as he finished the tattoo, something unexpected happened. Clara looked at herself in the mirror, and instead of the usual expression of triumph, of self-congratulation, she seemed at peace. She smiled softly, then turned to him.

"Thank you," she said simply, her eyes locking onto his.

Sebastian froze. Something about her gaze made him feel...unsettled. He had expected fear, or at least the usual awe people gave him when he revealed the final result. But Clara was different.

She knew.

Before he could react, she spoke again. "You think you're the only one who decides who deserves life and who doesn't? I know what you've been doing."

Sebastian's heart raced. How could she know? He hadn't made a mistake. She couldn't have known about the others, about his secret.

But Clara's smile widened. "You've been marking people with your judgments, Sebastian. And now, I'm marking you."

In an instant, he felt it—the sharp prick of a needle in his neck. The poison coursed through his veins, the world around him spinning as his vision blurred. He tried to stand, but his limbs no longer obeyed him. Clara's face loomed over him as his body succumbed to the drug.

"I'm freeing you, too," Clara whispered as he faded into darkness. "From your sins."

As Sebastian's last breath left him, he realized the ultimate lesson: no one escapes judgment. Not even the ones who think they hold the power.

The Librarian's Secret

Martha Whitaker had always found solace in silence. The hushed whispers between rows of books, the gentle rustle of pages turning—these were the sounds that calmed her restless mind. She had been the head librarian at the town's local library for over two decades, a position she had worked hard to attain. To everyone around her, she was a quiet, unassuming woman. She greeted patrons with a soft smile, guided them to the books they sought, and answered questions with a gentle patience that made her beloved in the community. But no one knew what simmered beneath the surface.

Books had always fascinated her. Not just the stories they told, but the power they held. The way words could influence, shape minds, and—if used correctly—control the fates of those who read them. For years, Martha had been careful, selecting books that could lead her down a path of control and manipulation. She had started small, leaving certain books where the right people could find them. And when they did, the stories inside would become a blueprint for their demise.

Her first victim had been an unsuspecting college student named Anna. Anna had come into the library one afternoon, lost in the aisles of fiction, searching for something to take her mind off her impending exams. Martha had watched her from across the room, quietly observing. Anna had seemed like the perfect candidate—young, ambitious, and eager to prove herself. Martha had known that this hunger for success would make Anna vulnerable to the suggestion she was about to plant.

Martha carefully selected a book from the shelf, a crime novel where the protagonist took extreme measures to achieve success, even at the cost of others' lives. She knew the story would appeal to Anna—after all, hadn't she heard her speak of her competitive spirit and her desire to rise above the rest? It was subtle, but she left the book prominently displayed on the counter when Anna came to check out her other selections. The title alone was enough to spark curiosity.

Over the following weeks, Martha observed Anna's behavior. She watched as the young woman devoured the book, her obsession growing with each chapter. Martha smiled to herself. It didn't take long before Anna started to mimic the protagonist's ruthless drive. She began to cut corners, cheat on her assignments, and alienate her friends—all in the name of ambition. But it wasn't enough. The story had planted a seed in Anna's mind, and soon, that seed blossomed into something darker.

Martha's intuition proved true. A week later, Anna was caught in a scandal that ruined her academic career. But that wasn't enough for Martha. She needed to ensure that the message of the book lived on, that it didn't just shape her victim's behavior but led her to an inevitable downfall. So, she watched closely, keeping her distance as Anna's desperation grew. Martha had selected the next book in the sequence—a psychological thriller about a character whose life unraveled because of a single, irreversible mistake. It was the perfect follow-up.

By the time Anna's life had spiraled, Martha had already planned the next move. She watched as Anna's mental state deteriorated, watched her buckle under the pressure. One evening, after Anna had read the final chapter, she came into the library one last time, her face pale and empty, her eyes unfocused. Martha approached her, offering a soft but knowing smile. Anna had no idea that the books she had picked had led her to this point.

As Anna left the library that night, she walked home in a haze, unaware that Martha had set her life on a predetermined course. The book had been the catalyst, and the final step was just around the corner. That night, Anna made the ultimate choice. She stepped in front of a moving car.

Martha wasn't shocked. In fact, she was pleased. She had orchestrated it all, guided Anna down a path she could not return from. It wasn't murder in the traditional sense. No. It was more subtle than that. She had planted the ideas, left the clues, and watched as her victim played her part.

But Martha was careful. She never left a trace. She didn't need to. The police ruled Anna's death as a tragic accident. No one would question the quiet librarian who spent her days amongst the stacks. She could move on to the next victim.

Her next target was a middle-aged man named Robert, a regular at the library who had recently fallen on hard times after losing his job. He came in frequently to escape his stress, always browsing self-help books and motivational literature. Robert was vulnerable, broken, and Martha saw an opportunity. She selected a book on redemption and second chances—about a man who turned his life around after making an irreversible mistake. The message was clear: anyone could change, but only if they took the hardest road.

She left the book on the counter one morning when Robert came in. As always, he picked it up, curious about the promise of transformation. Martha watched from behind a shelf as he checked out the book, knowing it would be his undoing. Over the next few weeks, she tracked his progress, pleased to see him devouring the pages, soaking in the philosophy of "starting over" that the book espoused. Robert started to take risks—attempting to reconcile with old business partners, pushing boundaries he had never dared to cross before. He believed in the false hope the book offered, believing that somehow, he could return to the man he once was.

But Martha knew the truth. The book was a setup. She had picked it specifically because she knew the protagonist's "second chance" was doomed from the beginning. Robert, in his pursuit of redemption, lost touch with reality. He made impulsive decisions that led him into a business deal that left him financially ruined. The pressure became too much. His desperation and belief in his own transformation led to a final, tragic mistake—a fatal heart attack, brought on by stress and overwhelming guilt.

The police, of course, found no foul play. Robert's death was ruled natural. No one suspected the quiet librarian, who continued to smile gently as people came and went from the library. She had planted the idea, she had guided him down a path that led him to his end, and no one would ever know. She had left no trace of her manipulation. It was beautiful. It was art.

Martha's power grew with each life she controlled. She had perfected the craft of psychological death. But soon, she started to realize something—she had become addicted to the power, to the control. She began to crave more—more victims, more lives to shape. But there was one problem: she had grown bored. The thrill of orchestrating deaths was no longer enough. She needed something bigger, something more.

One day, a new patron came into the library. Her name was Elizabeth, and she seemed different from the others. Elizabeth had a calm, confident air about her, an aura that made Martha uneasy. Elizabeth didn't come for the usual self-help books or novels. She asked for philosophy—books about the human condition, the ethics of life and death. Martha watched her closely, her curiosity piqued.

It didn't take long for Martha to realize that Elizabeth wasn't just another vulnerable person. She was someone who saw through Martha's facade. Elizabeth knew exactly what Martha was doing. And as Martha nervously approached her one afternoon, Elizabeth offered a simple smile.

"I've read all your books, Martha," she said. "And now it's time for you to read mine."

Elizabeth had been playing the same game. Only this time, it was Martha who was the victim. As the library's silence consumed her, Martha realized that the books she had once used to control others had now led her to her own inevitable end.

The Chef's Assistant

Lena had always admired the art of cooking from the moment she had set foot in a kitchen. As a young girl, she had spent countless hours watching her grandmother work, her hands moving with practiced precision as she created meals that left everyone at the table in awe. It wasn't just about the food; it was about the power. The way a single dish could change the atmosphere of a room, how it could elevate a person from being unnoticed to being revered.

By the time Lena had landed the job as a sous-chef in one of the city's most prestigious restaurants, she had earned every inch of respect she had garnered. She had worked her way up from small bistros, picking up every trick of the trade and every bit of knowledge she could find. But at *Le Ciel*, the Michelin-starred restaurant she now worked in, there was only one person who had the power: the head chef, Marco Vercelli.

Marco was everything Lena aspired to be: a culinary genius with a reputation that had stretched beyond the city's limits. His creations were masterpieces, each dish telling a story, each presentation perfect. He was a god in the kitchen, revered by his staff and adored by the guests. But to Lena, Marco was also the barrier between her and the title she so desperately craved. He was a man who took all the praise, all the attention, and all the glory. He was a man who stood in her way.

For years, she had been content with being his assistant, perfecting her skills, and learning the nuances of the culinary world. But as time went on, Lena's admiration for Marco began to sour into something darker. She realized she could do it all. She could run the kitchen just as well—better, even—and without Marco's ego getting in the way. But he wasn't going to step down. He never would. Not unless something drastic happened.

Lena knew she had to take matters into her own hands.

It started small. At first, she didn't think she was doing anything wrong. A little bit of seasoning in his coffee, just enough to make him feel off balance, to make him second-guess himself. Then, a bit of extra salt in his soup, so subtle that it wouldn't be noticed immediately, but just enough to cause a delay in his energy and focus. It was harmless at first. Just enough to give her the advantage, just enough to make her appear more capable without raising suspicion.

Marco's health started to decline. He complained about headaches, fatigue, and strange stomach pains, but the doctors couldn't find anything wrong. The team at *Le Ciel* attributed it to stress, the pressure of running a top-tier restaurant, but Lena knew better. She watched, ever so carefully, as Marco grew weaker with each passing week. She would always be there to pick up the slack, to show her brilliance when it mattered most, all the while making sure that he remained just a little too sick to perform at his best.

The kitchen began to notice the changes. Marco's once-immaculate dishes started to slip. There were minor errors, a burnt edge here, a missed flavor there. The staff whispered, some of them concerned, others intrigued by the sudden shift. They all respected Lena, though—she was the backbone of the operation now. She kept things running smoothly. When Marco wasn't able to make it in for a shift due to his "illness," it was Lena who took the reins, filling in for him with remarkable skill. The restaurant's reviews were still glowing, but it was becoming clear that something had shifted, and it wasn't just Marco's health.

One night, Marco's decline reached its peak. He was rushed to the hospital after collapsing in the middle of dinner service, unable to continue overseeing the kitchen. Lena, of course, was there when the staff panicked, stepping in and taking over without hesitation. She knew it would be only a matter of time before Marco's absence became permanent. She could already taste the triumph, feel the title she had long coveted slipping into her hands.

It wasn't long before Marco's condition was declared critical. He was placed in a medically induced coma, and the doctors didn't hold out much hope. They spoke of organ failure, of how his body was slowly shutting down. But Lena knew the truth. She had orchestrated it all. The poisoning, the slow, calculated build-up to this moment. She had done it in such a way that no one would ever suspect foul play. After all, what would anyone think? A chef, suffering from the stress of his job, running himself ragged until his body couldn't take it anymore. It was the perfect crime.

The day Marco died, Lena was promoted to head chef. She had earned it, no one could argue that. The restaurant continued to thrive under her leadership, and her reputation grew as the culinary world took notice of her brilliance. She was everything Marco had been, but without the flaws, without the ego. She was the perfect chef, admired and adored. The stars of *Le Ciel* continued to shine, but now, it was her name that was praised in the reviews, her face that appeared on the covers of magazines.

But as the months passed, Lena began to feel the weight of her success. The satisfaction that had initially filled her now felt like a hollow shell. She had achieved everything she had wanted—Marco's job, his glory, the life she had dreamed of—but something was missing. She had worked so hard to eliminate him, to take his place, but now that she was there, she couldn't shake the feeling that it wasn't hers to keep.

Lena had always believed she deserved the title, that she was the better chef, the one who could take *Le Ciel* to even greater heights. But now, she saw the truth. She had wanted the position, yes, but what she hadn't realized was that Marco's genius had always been in his ability to inspire those around him. He had created the legacy that Lena had now inherited. She hadn't built it herself. She had taken it, and in doing so, she had lost the one thing that made it meaningful.

The guilt gnawed at her, and soon, the realization set in. No matter how much she achieved, no matter how much acclaim she received, it wasn't enough. Marco had been the heart of the restaurant. His absence left a void that Lena couldn't fill, no matter how many accolades she received. In her quest for the title, she had destroyed the very thing that had made it worth having.

The lessons she had learned in the kitchen weren't just about technique or flavor; they were about power, control, and the cost of ambition. But in the end, Lena realized too late that taking the throne was never as satisfying as earning it. And now, all that was left was a restaurant filled with empty echoes and a kitchen that, despite her best efforts, could never truly replace what she had taken.

The Hit-and-Run Killer

Chloe Matthews was always the calm one. The one who never raised her voice, who always thought before she spoke, who could make even the most stressful situations feel manageable. She worked as a graphic designer, her days spent quietly at her computer, manipulating colors and images to craft the perfect designs for her clients. Her colleagues admired her for her professionalism, her collected demeanor. But no one truly knew Chloe. They didn't see the restless, gnawing emptiness inside her. They didn't understand the deep, insatiable need for control that drove her every decision.

Chloe had never been particularly cruel. In fact, she had always prided herself on being polite, kind, even empathetic. But over time, she began to feel as though the world around her was out of control—chaotic, messy, full of people who didn't deserve the space they took up. It wasn't that Chloe thought she was better than anyone; it was just that some people, in her eyes, simply didn't belong. They were reckless, selfish, or just plain ignorant. She found herself becoming increasingly irritated by their presence. Their loud voices, their careless actions, their thoughtlessness—it all grated on her nerves.

It started one evening when Chloe was driving home from work. She had just finished a long, tedious project for a client, her mind exhausted but still buzzing with the desire for something more. As she passed through a quiet intersection, a man on a bicycle swerved into her path. The light was green, and there was no way she could stop in time. Her foot hovered over the brake, but something within her snapped. Without a second thought, she hit the gas and struck him. The sound of the collision was dull, but she felt it—she felt the life leaving his body, felt the weight of his death settle in her car. But there was no panic. No remorse. Chloe just drove on, as if nothing had happened.

The next morning, the news reported the incident: a hit-and-run. The cyclist had died from his injuries, and the police were searching for the driver. But Chloe didn't worry. She knew exactly what to do. She washed the car, cleaned the blood off her bumper, and carefully erased all traces of her involvement. She didn't even think twice about it. The police would never find her. The man was just another victim, another statistic, his life barely a blip on the radar.

Weeks went by, and the incident faded from the public's memory. Chloe couldn't shake the sense of power she had felt. It was as though she had taken control of a situation that could have been chaotic and turned it into something clean, something final. No one had been able to touch her. The quiet satisfaction lingered, and soon, she found herself craving it.

Over the next several months, Chloe planned her next strike. She didn't need to plan for long—there were always people who didn't deserve to take up space. She began to target those who irritated her most. The young woman talking loudly on her phone in the grocery store parking lot, oblivious to the world around her. The man who had yelled at a cashier for making a mistake, his anger spilling over into something ugly. Chloe was methodical in her choices. She picked people who were selfish, thoughtless, or just plain rude. In her mind, they didn't belong in her world.

Each hit was executed with precision. Chloe would wait for the perfect moment—when the person was distracted, when they weren't paying attention. A quick nudge of the accelerator, a brief collision, and then she would drive away without a trace. She always made sure to cover her tracks, to erase every shred of evidence. The police were left clueless, just as they had been after the first incident. No one had any idea who was behind the deaths. Chloe had become an expert at this dark game.

But with every kill, Chloe grew more confident. She began to push the limits. She started to choose more dangerous targets—people who were in positions of power, who she believed were abusing their influence. A well-known businessman who had been involved in multiple scandals. A politician whose policies she despised. These were people who had too much power, who had used their influence to trample others. Chloe decided it was time for them to be taken down.

The businessman was the first. Chloe had followed him for days, studying his routine, waiting for the perfect opportunity. She found him walking out of a fancy restaurant one night, his back turned as he checked his phone. Chloe drove by slowly, her eyes locked on him, and without hesitation, she swerved, knocking him to the ground. It was swift, calculated. She sped away, her heart racing with exhilaration.

The politician came next. Chloe had been watching her for weeks, waiting for the right moment. One evening, the woman was walking from her car to her office building. Chloe saw her crossing the street, her attention diverted by something on her phone. It was an easy target. Chloe pulled up, hit the gas, and struck her without remorse.

By now, Chloe had perfected the process. She was untouchable, her actions flawless. The news reported the incidents, but no one could find a connection between the deaths. She had become a ghost, a phantom passing through the world without leaving a trace.

But then came a twist she hadn't anticipated. Chloe didn't notice the shadow that had been following her—the one person who had been watching her from the very beginning. It was a detective named Sarah Turner, a woman who had been investigating the hit-and-run cases from the start. Sarah had been suspicious of the pattern, the odd sense of finality that surrounded each death. There were no witnesses, no surveillance footage, and no real leads. But there was something about the precision of each incident, something about the way each victim seemed to be hand-picked, that had caught Sarah's attention.

One night, as Chloe was leaving the restaurant after another successful kill, she noticed a car following her. She didn't think much of it, assuming it was just another driver on the road. But the car stayed close, tailing her through the streets. Chloe's heart began to race. For the first time, she felt exposed. She turned down a few side streets, hoping to lose the car, but it followed her every move.

Finally, Chloe made a sharp turn into a quiet alley, and the car stopped behind her. She quickly put the car in park and stepped out, but as she did, she saw Sarah Turner standing in front of her. The detective's face was calm, collected, but her eyes told a different story. She had been waiting for this moment.

"Your game is over, Chloe," Sarah said, her voice steady. "You've been too careful, too precise, but you made one mistake. You got greedy. You thought you could keep going forever, but nothing stays hidden forever."

Chloe's breath caught in her throat. She had been so confident, so sure of herself. But now, as she faced the detective, she realized the terrible truth—she had let her own hubris blind her. In her need to control, in her desire to rid the world of those she deemed unworthy, she had forgotten the most important rule of all: no one is truly invisible.

As Sarah approached, Chloe realized that her reign of terror had come to an end. The twisted satisfaction that had once filled her now turned to panic. There was no escape this time, no more victims to manipulate. She had driven her car too far, and now she was about to pay the price.

The Wedding Guest

Lila always knew how to make an entrance. She had perfected the art of slipping into high society events without anyone noticing her absence when it was time to leave. The sound of clinking champagne glasses, the sparkle of wedding gowns, and the opulence of endless tables stacked high with food had always fascinated her. For most people, weddings were about love and celebration. But for Lila, they were opportunities—moments where everything was ripe for the taking.

She'd learned a long time ago that love wasn't something she would ever have. She had never been the center of anyone's world, not like those bright, shining brides or the charming grooms who were adored by their friends and families. Instead, Lila had watched from the sidelines, her eyes trained on the lives of others. She learned quickly that it wasn't just enough to want attention; she had to take it. And what better way than to step into the perfect picture of happiness—weddings.

She didn't crash weddings out of desperation. No, that was too messy, too careless. Lila had a plan. She would slip in unnoticed, work her charm, and weave herself into the life of someone special. It was always a man—someone with wealth, influence, or status—and she would get close enough to make them hers, if only for a night. They would fall for her beauty, her allure, her delicate touch. She would lead them into a private conversation, a stolen moment, where they would confess their deepest desires.

And then she would make her move.

The first wedding Lila attended was a grand affair—tall chandeliers hung from the ceiling, flowers in every corner, and guests who were too busy basking in their own joy to notice her slipping in like a shadow. Her dress was perfect, the one she always wore for these kinds of events.

It was deep red, bold enough to draw attention, but not too obvious. She knew how to blend into the background while simultaneously standing out. That was part of her charm.

She found her target early on: Daniel, the groom. He was handsome, rich, and his eyes wandered a little too often to the women around him, especially to Lila. She could tell he wasn't truly invested in his new bride. Lila could see the signs—the way he smiled, the way his fingers lingered just a little too long when handing over a drink. A man like Daniel was always looking for an escape, and Lila was more than happy to provide it.

She waited until the reception was in full swing, the noise of the celebration and the rhythm of the music swallowing up everything. With a practiced move, she found herself standing next to Daniel, her soft laugh filling the space between them. He was polite at first, a little hesitant, but Lila knew just how to push his buttons. She talked about the wedding, the meaning of the vows, the promises made between strangers who hadn't yet been tested by time. The conversation turned personal, and Daniel began to confide in her. He was in love, yes, but something was missing. He wanted more than just the façade of a perfect marriage. His eyes shifted nervously, but they didn't leave her. That was when she knew it was time to make him believe he had found it.

Lila led him outside to the balcony under the guise of wanting some fresh air. The night air was crisp, and the sounds of the party grew faint. They spoke quietly, and then, as she predicted, Daniel made the mistake of reaching for her hand. She let him. With a soft smile, she turned it into something more. She leaned into him, letting her lips brush his ear, whispering promises of a night away from everything, of the things that could never be spoken of in the open. He was hooked.

But the game wasn't over yet.

Lila had planned this night meticulously, as she did with every one of her "escapes." She had slipped something into the champagne earlier—a drug, one that would take effect slowly, but surely. A few minutes later, she could see it. Daniel's movements grew sluggish, his words slurred. He leaned against the balcony railing, his eyes unfocused as he tried to fight the effects. But it was too late. The drug was taking hold. He would fall unconscious soon, and once he did, she would make sure there was no coming back for him.

She walked him back inside, keeping him steady on his feet as the room spun around him. By the time they reached the bathroom, Lila had already prepared everything. The pipe was easy to tamper with—she had done it so many times before. As Daniel struggled to stay upright, she guided his hand to the sink, the water flowing smoothly. He had no idea that she had taken the water and laced it with a stronger dose of the drug. The rest was simple. She placed her hand over his mouth when he collapsed into the sink, drowning him in a death that no one would ever be able to trace back to her.

It was clean, efficient. She slipped away into the crowd, leaving behind nothing but the memory of a man lost in the celebration of his wedding. By morning, the police would report it as an unfortunate accident—drunken behavior, an unfortunate fall, a tragic end. His bride, devastated, would never suspect the truth.

But Lila didn't stop there. Daniel's death was just another step in her game. She had already begun planning the next wedding she would crash, the next victim who would fall for her charm. There was always another groom, always another life to take.

But things began to shift after her fourth wedding. This one was different. She had targeted another man, but this time something went wrong. She had made her move, seduced him in the same way she always did, led him away from the crowd. But this time, he wasn't as easy to manipulate. His name was Thomas, and as she whispered in his ear, promising him everything he desired, she saw something she hadn't expected: fear.

Thomas wasn't overwhelmed by her beauty or her power. He wasn't looking for a way out of his marriage. He had seen through her act, and instead of falling for her, he laughed.

"You're not the first woman who's tried this," he said, his voice low but steady. "You think you're clever, don't you? But I know exactly who you are. You've been playing this game for a while."

Lila froze. Her heart raced. She tried to regain control, but it was too late. Thomas wasn't just another target. He had been following her for weeks, investigating her carefully. He had seen through her façade, and now he knew. The hunter had become the hunted.

As the realization dawned on her, Thomas pulled out a small phone and snapped a picture. Lila's world came crashing down. The trail of bodies, the careful planning—it had all been for nothing. The game she thought she controlled was no longer hers to play.

The last thing Lila saw was Thomas's smirk as he sent the picture to the authorities. The game was over.

The Crafty Killer

Maggie Porter had always loved crafting. From a young age, she found solace in the quiet repetition of creating something beautiful with her hands. She started small, making jewelry and knitting scarves to sell at local flea markets, but over time, her business had grown. Soon, she had a loyal following, customers who sought her out at craft fairs and online. She prided herself on her work, each piece a testament to her skill, her attention to detail. What people didn't know, however, was that Maggie's true craft wasn't in making jewelry or pottery—it was in making herself indispensable to people, only to twist that trust into something far darker.

Maggie had always been the quiet one, the one who blended in, but that gave her the perfect cover. People didn't suspect the woman who smiled so sweetly, who spoke so kindly. They didn't realize how calculated she was, how adept she was at reading people's weaknesses. She'd learned long ago that people, no matter how kind or honest they seemed, were often searching for something. And Maggie, with her sharp mind and understanding of human nature, could always find that thing. Whether it was loneliness, ambition, or fear of failure, Maggie knew exactly how to exploit it.

Her first victim had been Donna, a fellow craftsperson who ran a small, charming shop selling handmade candles. Donna's business had been struggling, and Maggie, ever the empath, saw an opportunity. She visited the shop under the guise of being a customer, complimenting the candles, listening to Donna's troubles. Maggie knew how to make her feel understood, how to position herself as a friend, a mentor, someone who could help. Soon, Maggie was offering advice on marketing, helping Donna with her social media, and even offering to take over some of the management tasks that were weighing Donna down.

As Donna trusted her more, Maggie's role in the business grew. She took on more responsibility, showing up at the shop regularly, offering her expertise. Donna, exhausted and overwhelmed, was grateful for the help. Maggie made it seem so easy—she was smart, driven, and organized in a way that Donna could never be. Slowly, Donna began to fade into the background of her own business, allowing Maggie to take more control.

It was only when Maggie started taking more liberties with the finances, moving money around without asking, that things began to feel off. But by then, Donna was too dependent on Maggie's help to question anything. She was tired, worn out, and believed Maggie was the key to the success her shop had always lacked.

One evening, as the store was closing, Maggie offered to help Donna clear out some of the stock and rearrange the displays. It was then that Maggie made her move. She had spent weeks carefully poisoning Donna's drinks, a slow, insidious process, making it seem like fatigue or stress was causing the woman's growing weakness. On that final night, Maggie had dosed Donna's drink with a fatal amount of something that would make her collapse without a struggle.

By the time the paramedics arrived, it was too late. Donna was dead. The police ruled it as an unfortunate heart attack, brought on by stress. No one suspected Maggie. She had worked her way into Donna's life so smoothly, so subtly, that no one could see the darkness behind her kindness.

With Donna out of the picture, Maggie was free to take over the shop. She had already transferred ownership of the business into her name while Donna had been too weak to notice, and now, she had an established shop with a loyal customer base. Business boomed under her management. The shop's sales skyrocketed as Maggie carefully curated new products and marketed them in ways Donna had never imagined. The money flowed easily, and Maggie's confidence grew.

As her success continued, Maggie realized there were more opportunities to seize. She didn't just want to run a single shop; she wanted to own a network of businesses. So, she set her sights on someone else—Lily, a young woman who owned a small but profitable handmade pottery studio. Lily had inherited her business from her grandmother and was struggling with modernizing the brand while keeping the personal touch intact. Maggie saw her vulnerability. She saw the uncertainty in Lily's eyes when they talked about her business, the fear of change. Maggie moved quickly.

She began visiting Lily's shop, admiring the pottery, asking questions about how Lily had gotten started. She offered advice—subtle suggestions that Lily took to heart. Maggie, knowing how to appeal to Lily's insecurities, convinced her that she could help her expand the business. She offered to take over the marketing, to handle the orders and the logistics, all while leaving the creative aspects to Lily. At first, Lily was hesitant, but Maggie's charm and the way she made her feel capable, made her feel like the business was finally going to thrive, won her over.

Once again, Maggie worked her way into Lily's life. As the months passed, she became more indispensable, more trusted. She pushed Lily to take on larger orders, to expand beyond the small local market. And just as before, Maggie began to manipulate the business's finances, moving funds around to make the shop's success look like Lily's hard work, even though Maggie was the one behind the scenes making all the key decisions.

One day, after a particularly successful business deal that Maggie had orchestrated, she invited Lily to a celebratory dinner. It was in the middle of the meal when Maggie slipped something into Lily's wine, a fast-acting poison that would cause her to fall unconscious, and from there, Maggie could finish what she had started.

The next morning, Lily was found in her apartment, having "passed out from exhaustion" after a long day. The authorities were called, and Maggie, once again, had made sure her tracks were covered. The cause of death was ruled as a sudden heart failure due to stress, and Maggie, as always, slipped away without suspicion.

With Lily gone, Maggie took full control of the pottery studio, just as she had with Donna's business. She streamlined operations, expanded the product line, and sold off Lily's original creations for a small fortune. In a matter of months, Maggie had taken over not just one, but two thriving businesses.

But as Maggie looked around at the success she had created, something inside her began to stir. She felt the emptiness creeping back, the realization that no matter how much she took, it would never fill the void inside her. She had everything now—money, power, influence—but none of it was truly hers. It had all come at the expense of others.

One evening, as she sat in the lavish office of her new expanded studio, her phone buzzed. It was a message from an unknown number. She opened it, her eyes widening as she read the short text: "You won't get away with it forever. The truth is coming."

For the first time, Maggie felt the chill of fear. She had made her success by erasing the people who stood in her way, but now, she wondered who was watching her, who had been paying attention to the carefully crafted illusion she had built. As the walls closed in around her, she realized that no one could stay hidden forever—and that maybe, just maybe, it was her turn to become the next victim of the darkness she had created.

The Infiltrator

Grace had always been a quiet observer, watching the world from the periphery, staying hidden in plain sight. She had spent years perfecting the art of blending in, learning how to wear the masks that the world demanded, how to be the person everyone expected her to be. But beneath the calm exterior, there was a dark, simmering rage that she could never quite contain. It wasn't the kind of rage that people could see—it was subtle, insidious, and it festered within her, feeding on the stories she heard, the injustices she witnessed.

Grace knew what it was like to suffer. She had known pain, humiliation, betrayal. She had felt the sting of a broken heart and the crushing weight of loneliness. But what set her apart from the others was that she never allowed herself to heal. She let the pain linger, nourished it, let it grow into something more dangerous. She found a twisted kind of solace in her anger, in the stories of women who had been wronged.

That was why she joined the support groups.

At first, it seemed innocent enough. Grace had heard about the group from a friend—women who gathered together to share their experiences, to support each other after they had been victimized, abused, neglected. She knew the value of community, the way it could help you feel heard, understood, like you were not alone. It was perfect. She could listen, nod sympathetically, and hide in the shadows of their pain. But for Grace, it wasn't about healing. It was about something else entirely. It was about the power she could extract from their vulnerability.

Grace started attending the group sessions regularly. She would sit quietly at first, offering little more than a few words of encouragement. Her presence was calming, almost soothing. She blended into the background, allowing the others to take center stage as they bared their souls. Each woman had a story—stories of violent partners, oppressive families, crushing betrayals. Grace listened carefully, absorbing every detail, memorizing the names, the places, the faces, the histories. They didn't know it, but each woman's trauma was a puzzle piece for Grace to fit into her own sick game.

She took careful notes in her mind, noting where each woman lived, who they were close to, and what made them vulnerable. She asked just enough questions to earn their trust, never too much to arouse suspicion. Slowly, she became a fixture in their lives. She showed up early, stayed late, offered rides when needed, made herself indispensable. She was the quiet confidante, the one who didn't ask for anything in return, the one who would be there when no one else was.

It wasn't long before Grace started to pick her targets. She had learned how to separate the weak from the strong, how to spot the women who could easily be manipulated, those who were still too raw, too fragile, to protect themselves from someone like her. There was Lily, a woman in her thirties who had been abused by her husband for years. Her eyes were always downcast, her shoulders hunched, like she was carrying the weight of the world on her back. Then there was Natalie, a young woman in her twenties who had fled a toxic family, only to find herself trapped in a cycle of abusive relationships. She wore the scars of betrayal on her arms, and Grace could see the desperation in her eyes.

But it was the story of Rachel that fascinated her the most. Rachel had grown up in a religious household, her father a domineering figure who had controlled every aspect of her life. She had finally escaped, only to find herself in an equally suffocating relationship with a man who, on the surface, seemed perfect. But underneath, he was a monster. Rachel's face was always pained, like she was living in a constant state of fear. Her voice trembled when she spoke, as if she was afraid to say the wrong thing.

Grace knew that Rachel was the one she would take first. She learned everything she could about her—the apartment she lived in, the job she worked, the places she visited. The more Grace learned, the more she could sense the cracks in Rachel's armor. She was so close to breaking, and that was when Grace would strike.

One evening, after a particularly intense group session, Grace offered to walk Rachel home. Rachel, always eager for someone to talk to, accepted gratefully. They walked in silence at first, the air thick with unspoken words. Then, as they approached Rachel's building, Grace finally spoke. "You know, you don't have to keep living like this. You don't have to keep letting him control you."

Rachel's eyes flickered nervously, but Grace continued, her voice soft, coaxing. "I can help you. I can make sure he never hurts you again. All you have to do is trust me."

Rachel looked at her, doubt clouding her expression, but there was something in Grace's eyes, something that made her believe, if only for a moment, that she could finally be free. That night, Rachel confided in Grace about the last violent incident, the one that had pushed her to the brink. Grace offered her a solution, a way out. She promised Rachel that she could help her leave him, start fresh.

But Grace wasn't offering freedom. She was offering a death sentence.

The next day, Rachel's body was found, hidden in an alley a few blocks from her apartment. The police quickly ruled it as a tragic accident. There was no sign of forced entry, no signs of struggle. It was as though Rachel had simply wandered off into the night and met her fate. Grace made sure of it. She had learned enough about Rachel's abuser to make sure the investigation would go nowhere. Her plan had worked perfectly.

Grace didn't stop there. Each woman she had gotten close to—Lily, Natalie, even others in the group—became part of her twisted scheme. She was careful, precise, always leaving behind just enough clues to make sure the world saw them as victims of circumstance, never suspecting the woman who had been right under their noses. She was the helper, the savior, the friend. But in truth, she was the architect of their demise.

It wasn't until Grace turned her attention to the last woman—Samantha—that the cracks in her plan began to show. Samantha had been part of the group for only a few months, but she was different. She was sharp, self-aware, and more than just a little suspicious. When Grace tried to manipulate her, to push her into a corner like she had with the others, Samantha began to fight back. She started asking questions, noticing inconsistencies in Grace's stories.

One evening, as Grace walked Samantha home, she realized the terrible truth—Samantha had been watching her too. She had pieced it together. The way each victim had disappeared, the way Grace had always been there, just a little too close. Samantha had already gone to the authorities.

Grace didn't run. She didn't need to. By the time the police arrived, Samantha was dead, lying in a pool of blood in an alley near her apartment. Grace had made sure that the truth would never come to light. The lesson was simple—no matter how carefully you craft your plan, someone is always watching, and eventually, they'll see through the lies.

In the end, Grace realized that her desire to control had only brought her closer to her own downfall. She had taken the lives of the very women she had once tried to understand, and in the end, it was her own reflection that betrayed her.

The Art Collector

Elena Harris had always been fascinated by the concept of art, not just as a form of expression, but as a commodity. The brushstrokes, the splashes of color, the curves and lines—all of it was beautiful, yes, but even more so, it was valuable. Art was something that could be owned, displayed, and consumed by the right people in the right circles. As a young woman with no particular talent of her own, Elena had realized early on that the true power in the art world didn't belong to the creators. It belonged to those who controlled the narrative. And Elena, with her sharp mind and cold ambition, knew exactly how to create that narrative.

She had learned to identify those who were on the brink of greatness, the artists whose works were still raw, unrefined, but brimming with potential. There was something magnetic about them, a quality that drew her in and made them easy to manipulate. Elena didn't care about their stories, their struggles, their lives. She cared about their art, and how she could claim it for herself.

It started with Thomas Kline, a painter known for his stark, abstract landscapes. His works were revolutionary, but his success had been slow to come. He was a quiet man, alone in his studio, completely unaware that Elena had been watching him for months. He had no one. No significant relationships, no network of connections to elevate him. He was the perfect target. Elena introduced herself at a gallery opening, complimenting his work with the kind of praise that only someone with deep knowledge could offer. She spoke of his compositions, his use of color, and his future. She made him feel seen, understood.

Within weeks, Elena had worked her way into his life, becoming his trusted confidante, his muse. He trusted her with his thoughts, his sketches, his plans. He showed her unfinished pieces, works he had yet to display to the world. Elena had already begun the process of positioning herself as his greatest ally, the one who would launch him into the art world's elite circles. But Elena had her own plan. She needed him, but only for as long as it took to take what she wanted.

The first death was the easiest. Thomas had been alone in his apartment when Elena visited him under the pretense of discussing his next exhibition. She offered him a glass of wine, laced with enough sleeping pills to knock him out for hours. When he was unconscious, she carefully rearranged the room, placing him at his easel, the unfinished landscape in front of him. It looked like the work of a man lost in his art, a tragic artist who had died before he could complete his masterpiece. Elena made sure to leave a bottle of pills in plain sight, as though it were a suicide, a man overwhelmed by the weight of his own genius.

The art world mourned Thomas Kline's tragic death. His works skyrocketed in value, and Elena, the artist's closest friend, became a key figure in his posthumous success. She was hailed as a visionary, someone who had recognized his potential before the world had. She began to make a name for herself in the circles of collectors and critics, gaining access to exhibitions, private viewings, and more artists. She learned to play the game better, to position herself as a champion of the unknown, the underappreciated.

Her next victim was a sculptor named Gabriel Serrano, whose delicate, minimalist creations had begun to garner attention. Gabriel was an eccentric, his mind always preoccupied with new ideas, and Elena saw a man just as vulnerable as Thomas had been. She ingratiated herself with him, offering support and guidance, slowly worming her way into his world. Gabriel, unlike Thomas, was not as easily fooled, but Elena was patient. She played the long game, drawing him into her web. Eventually, he began to trust her completely, even allowing her to take a more active role in his projects. Elena knew it wouldn't take long before his art would belong to her.

One night, Gabriel invited her to his studio to unveil a new piece he had been working on. It was a stunning marble sculpture, an abstract human form that seemed to reach out for something unattainable. As they admired it together, Elena's thoughts turned to the inevitable. She had already planted the idea in Gabriel's mind that he needed to push boundaries, to go further with his art. But what Gabriel didn't realize was that he had crossed his own boundary. Elena had already made sure the marble dust had been laced with something far more deadly. Gabriel's breath became shallow, his vision blurred, and as he collapsed in front of the sculpture, Elena ensured that his final moments were witnessed by no one but the art he had created. Once again, it was a tragedy. A tortured soul lost to the pressures of his craft.

Elena immediately claimed Gabriel's sculpture as her own work, calling it a tribute to him. She capitalized on the death of another brilliant artist, moving swiftly to market his pieces, positioning them as the final legacy of a visionary who had tragically passed. The more she took, the more powerful she became. The critics, the collectors, all praised her for recognizing the true worth of the artists she "championed." But Elena knew the truth: she was the one pulling the strings, the one orchestrating the tragedies that propelled her career.

Soon, Elena had access to the highest echelons of the art world. She was sought after by collectors and curators alike, her name synonymous with genius. She had amassed a fortune, a collection of works that were all attributed to the dead. No one suspected her—how could they? She had always been the quiet, supportive friend, the one who "understood the artist." But the moment was coming, the moment when the world would recognize her not just as an art promoter, but as an artist in her own right.

Then came the twist.

Elena's last move was a painter named Lisa Hale, a prodigy in the world of portraiture. Lisa's work was raw, emotional, and unlike anything the world had seen in years. She was the next big thing, and Elena knew it. Lisa, unlike the others, was sharp, suspicious, and driven. She never fully trusted Elena, but Elena was relentless. She spent months building the trust, playing the game just as she had with the others. But Lisa was too clever to fall for the same tricks.

One night, after a gallery opening where Elena was the center of attention, Lisa confronted her. "I know what you've done," Lisa said quietly, her voice steady. "I've been watching you."

For a moment, Elena's heart raced. She had no way out. Lisa knew too much. But then, to Elena's shock, Lisa smiled.

"You see," Lisa continued, "I've been using you, too."

Lisa had been one step ahead the entire time. She had been manipulating Elena into doing the very thing that would expose her. The final act of betrayal was simple: as Elena had done with the others, she had manipulated the situation to ensure Lisa's success—only this time, Lisa had been the one pulling the strings.

As Elena was arrested for her crimes, her carefully crafted empire began to crumble. The world that had once celebrated her was left in ruins. The lesson, however, was clear: even the most powerful manipulators can be outplayed when they believe they control the game.

The Party Girl

Serena Crawford had always been at the heart of every celebration. Her smile was radiant, her laughter infectious, and her presence, magnetic. She moved effortlessly through high society, always surrounded by the wealthiest and most influential people. Serena knew how to throw a party that would be remembered, an event where every detail was meticulously planned and executed. She had access to the kind of world most could only dream of—the glittering world of mansions, private jets, and champagne-filled evenings with the famous and the powerful. But beneath the glamorous facade, Serena had a darkness that no one ever saw.

For Serena, the lavish parties were more than just a means of enjoying herself. They were a hunting ground, a place where she could target the people who had everything. They had the money, the power, the status—and yet, to Serena, they were empty. She had spent years in their circles, watching them indulge in their wealth, their luxuries, all while they treated people like herself—people who had no inherited fortune, no influence, no legacy—as if they were beneath them. She knew how to play the game, how to make them feel special, how to fit into their world seamlessly. But secretly, Serena harbored a resentment for them that had festered, silently but steadily, for years.

She wanted more. And if they weren't going to give it to her, then she'd take it. She would rid herself of the people who had so carelessly lived lives that Serena could only dream of. She would manipulate their need for attention, their craving for admiration, and in the end, she would claim their world for herself.

The first time it happened, Serena had been at an exclusive gala, rubbing elbows with the city's elite. As usual, she was the life of the party, the woman everyone gravitated toward. She made the men laugh, charmed the women with her wit and beauty, and had the attention of the entire room. It was there that she met Richard Langley, a billionaire businessman whose name was on the lips of everyone in the room. He was charming, yes, but cold and calculating underneath, the kind of man who used his wealth to manipulate everyone around him. Serena had heard the stories—the way he treated his employees, the way he stepped on anyone who got in his way. Richard was a man who believed that his money could protect him from consequences.

Serena made sure he noticed her. She played the game as only she knew how, flattering him, making him feel like he was the most important man in the room. She knew just how to get him to lower his guard. By the time they were sitting in a quiet corner, sipping on expensive wine, Richard was entranced. He talked about his business ventures, his triumphs, and Serena listened intently, pretending to be fascinated by every word.

When the moment was right, she made her move. Serena had slipped the poison into his drink when he wasn't paying attention—just enough to make it seem like a heart attack or some other natural cause. She had researched the toxins, made sure that no one would ever be able to trace it back to her. She was a master at covering her tracks, and tonight would be no exception.

Richard took another sip of his wine, his eyes never leaving Serena's face. He was starting to feel light-headed, but he didn't realize what was happening. As the minutes ticked by, Serena could see the life draining from him, the realization that something was wrong creeping into his expression. The room was still alive with laughter and chatter, no one noticing Richard's slow collapse.

Within minutes, he slumped forward, his glass falling from his hand and shattering on the floor. People rushed to him, but it was too late. The paramedics who arrived a short time later pronounced him dead at the scene. The cause? Cardiac arrest, they said. Nothing out of the ordinary. Serena played the part of the concerned guest, offering her condolences and pretending to be shocked by the sudden tragedy. But inside, she felt a strange sense of satisfaction. She had rid herself of one more person who had thought they were untouchable.

The weeks that followed were a blur of headlines, funeral arrangements, and somber memorials. But Serena wasn't worried. No one suspected her. She was too charming, too well-liked. And, as the weeks turned into months, she found herself more ingrained in the circles that had once seemed so out of reach. Richard's death was ruled a tragic accident, and the world moved on, as it always did.

But Serena knew that the key to her success wasn't in simply enjoying the parties—it was in taking them over. She had already begun targeting other prominent figures in the socialite world, carefully choosing her next victim. There was Peter Madsen, a well-known philanthropist whose charity events were always the talk of the town. He had a reputation for being generous, for caring about causes that mattered, but Serena had learned the truth—he was a fraud, a man who made money from his charity work and used it as a front for his own selfish needs. Serena found the idea of eliminating him exhilarating.

The plan was much the same as Richard's. She ingratiated herself with him, played the perfect seductress, the caring woman who understood the weight of his responsibilities. They spent an evening together at one of his lavish events, and as they shared a private moment, she did it again. This time, it was a dose of a different poison, one that would mimic the symptoms of a stroke. Peter collapsed, just as Richard had, and the room erupted into panic. He died in a similar manner, leaving his wealth and his influence behind. Serena, of course, was the picture of grief, consoling his widow, comforting the guests, all while basking in the success of her latest "accident."

But Serena was careful this time. She had learned from her earlier mistake—she was getting too comfortable, too bold. The deaths of two prominent figures were starting to raise eyebrows, even in the circles where she operated. People were starting to whisper. And while no one could connect her directly to the deaths, Serena realized that she needed to be more strategic.

So she laid low for a while, staying out of the spotlight, building her influence more subtly. She took over smaller businesses, bought art, and infiltrated even more exclusive parties. The wealth she had accumulated from these deaths was substantial, and the respect she had in high society grew. It wasn't long before her name was synonymous with success in the circles she moved in. She had become an untouchable figure, someone who had everything—but she didn't realize that the power she had taken had slowly started to slip away.

One evening, after another successful gala, Serena received an anonymous message, a photo attached. The photo was of her, in the background of one of the events, standing next to Richard Langley, looking over his shoulder as he drank his poisoned wine. The note read simply: "You're not the only one playing the game."

Serena's heart stopped. It wasn't the first time she had seen this message, but it was the first time it had come so close. Someone was watching her, someone had been tracking her movements. She'd been so careful, so sure that no one could ever figure it out. But now, she knew—the game was over. The hunter had become the hunted, and it was only a matter of time before someone would expose her.

Serena had taken everything she wanted, but in the end, she had failed to see that someone else had always been waiting for the right moment to strike. The darkness she had unleashed would soon return to claim her.

The Angel of Death

Clara had always been drawn to the idea of helping others. Growing up in a small town, she had been raised to believe that kindness was the highest virtue. She spent her days volunteering in various roles—at the local food bank, in homeless shelters, and, most recently, at the hospice care center. She felt a quiet sense of pride in her work, knowing she was doing something important, even if the impact of her actions was often intangible. She wasn't just giving her time; she was giving her soul, she believed. But what began as a desire to do good soon twisted into something far darker.

At the hospice, Clara was surrounded by the dying—patients who had been given a limited time left to live, their bodies already ravaged by diseases that no medicine could cure. She helped care for them, made them comfortable, held their hands when they cried, and whispered reassurances when they feared their time was coming to an end. And while many of her fellow volunteers showed compassion, Clara's thoughts began to wander. She started to notice something about the patients she cared for—something that lingered in her mind long after her shifts were over.

These people were ready to die. Some were at peace with their fate, their lives drawn to an inevitable close. Others fought, clinging to whatever hope they had left, but Clara saw a different kind of suffering in them—the slow, painful decline that left their loved ones exhausted and broken. She began to think that maybe she could help them along, put an end to their suffering, but not out of mercy. No, that wasn't it at all. It was more selfish than that. It was about control. About taking the power from the disease and putting it into her hands.

The first time it happened, it was almost an accident. Mrs. Caldwell was an elderly woman who had been bedridden for months, her body withered from cancer. She had no family left, only a handful of nurses and volunteers who came to check on her. Clara, who had often been the one to sit with her, had grown fond of the woman. She could see the pain in Mrs. Caldwell's eyes every time she looked up at her, the way she tried to speak but could only manage whispers.

One night, Clara stayed late, sitting beside Mrs. Caldwell's bed, reading to her from a book of poems. Her hands trembled slightly as she held the page, and in the dim light, she noticed how ragged Mrs. Caldwell's breathing had become. The old woman's chest rose and fell with labored effort, her eyes fluttering as though fighting to stay open. Clara's thoughts turned dark, and for a moment, she felt an overwhelming urge to help her. Not help her by comforting her, not help her by holding her hand until the inevitable arrived. No. Clara's mind was clouded with something else entirely.

She glanced over at the bedside table, where the medication bottles were neatly arranged. It would be so simple, she thought. A small dose, a gentle push to ease her pain. She could give her the overdose that would stop her suffering. No one would even notice. Mrs. Caldwell wouldn't even feel it.

Clara hesitated. Then, without fully understanding why, she did it. She poured an extra dose of the morphine into the syringe and injected it into Mrs. Caldwell's IV. She watched, transfixed, as the elderly woman's breathing slowed, her frail body surrendering to the darkness. Clara sat quietly, her heart pounding, as the life left Mrs. Caldwell's body. The old woman's face relaxed, a soft smile on her lips as if, for the first time in years, she was at peace.

Clara stood up and carefully cleaned up the evidence, disposed of the syringe, and left the room, her footsteps silent on the tile floor. She didn't feel guilty. She didn't feel sad. No, instead, she felt something else—something she couldn't name but recognized immediately. Power. A feeling of accomplishment. She had done something. She had taken control, given an end to a life that had been left to decay.

The next morning, Mrs. Caldwell was found dead, the cause listed as complications from cancer. No one suspected foul play. Clara's calmness was her shield.

From that night forward, Clara began to do the same for others—only the ones she chose. She started small, carefully selecting the patients who were already on the brink, those who had no family, those whose bodies were too far gone to recover. She would visit them under the guise of offering comfort, holding their hands, offering them a few final words. Then, when the moment was right, she would inject them with an overdose of painkillers, slipping them quietly into the darkness.

She didn't know what she was doing. She didn't fully understand why she was doing it. But she didn't stop. With each patient, each victim, she felt more powerful, more in control. No one questioned her. After all, she was the volunteer. She was the one who cared.

It wasn't long before Clara started to enjoy her power. She didn't just target the ones who were at peace with death; she started to choose the ones who fought against it, the ones who begged for a cure, the ones who clung to the last threads of hope. These were the people she truly wanted to control. They had something she didn't—a drive, a will to live that she could manipulate, bend, and break. She enjoyed watching them struggle as she ended their lives, taking that final choice away from them.

But it was during one of her late-night shifts, as she moved from room to room, that Clara met someone who would change everything—William. He had been there for weeks, an elderly man with a sharp mind and a body worn by time. His family rarely visited, but he didn't seem bothered. He spent his days reading, and when Clara sat with him, he always had a wry smile for her, as though he knew something she didn't.

One night, Clara went into his room with the familiar syringe in hand, ready to end another life. But when she tried to speak with him, William's eyes flickered with awareness, as though he had been waiting for her.

"You're here for me, aren't you?" he asked, his voice weak but steady.

Clara froze. "What do you mean?"

He smiled faintly. "I've seen what you've done. You're not fooling anyone. You think you're giving them peace, but you're only feeding your own darkness."

Clara's heart skipped a beat. She felt a chill run through her. How did he know? How long had he known? But before she could react, he continued.

"I know why you do it. You don't care about mercy. You care about control. You've been using them, just like you've used yourself, trying to fill a void that can never be filled."

Clara backed away, the syringe shaking in her hands. Her mind raced. "You're wrong."

"No," William said softly, his eyes clear and piercing. "I'm not. You've taken everything you could, but it won't save you. It's never enough."

As Clara stood there, the weight of his words crashing over her, she realized the terrible truth. She had lived her entire life trying to control others, trying to fill a darkness within herself that she could never escape. And now, she was the one who had become trapped.

William's death came the next morning, peacefully, without Clara's interference. But for the first time, Clara felt the weight of what she had done—the emptiness, the unending cycle of trying to fill the void with the lives of others. She had never been the angel of mercy. She had only ever been the Angel of Death.

The Family Therapist

Dr. Claire Westbrook had built her career on the fragile trust of broken families. She was renowned in her community for her work as a family therapist, specializing in mediation for those at their lowest points—couples on the verge of divorce, parents and children locked in endless cycles of conflict, siblings who hadn't spoken to each other in years. She had a way with words, a gift for seeing the heart of things that most people missed. Her soothing voice and empathetic demeanor made her the go-to therapist for those who needed someone to listen, someone to guide them through their darkest times.

But Claire didn't just listen. She understood the power she held. Every family that walked through her door came with their own set of wounds, their own vulnerabilities, and Claire could feel it, deep within her. She didn't just see the tears; she saw the fractures, the faults, the cracks waiting to be widened. And as much as she played the role of the caring therapist, someone who wanted to help, Claire knew the truth: she was playing them. She could manipulate their emotions, drive wedges between them, fuel their pain and distrust, all under the guise of helping. She could make their lives worse—more fractured, more desperate—and in doing so, make them even more reliant on her. She had learned how to twist their emotions into a weapon, to destroy what little family they had left, and when it was all too much, when someone couldn't bear the weight of their own despair, she would be there, ready to offer a twisted solution.

The first time she realized how easy it was to control someone, to push them past the breaking point, was with the Marlowe family. They had come to her after their teenage son, Ethan, had started acting out—rebellion, violence, defiance. His mother, Evelyn, was at her wit's end, while his father, Mark, was distant and uninvolved. Claire saw the dynamic immediately: a mother desperate for control and affection, a father emotionally absent, and a son craving attention in the only ways he knew how. Claire knew exactly what to do.

She began by focusing on Mark. She told him, ever so gently, that he was the root of Ethan's problems, that his detachment had created a deep rift in the family. She made Mark feel guilty for his failure as a father, playing on his insecurities. As she watched his emotional walls crumble, Claire turned her attention to Evelyn, reinforcing her belief that Mark was emotionally distant, that he was neglecting her needs as a wife. Soon, Evelyn was convinced that their marriage was falling apart, that Mark didn't care about her or their son.

The sessions became a battlefield, with Claire in the middle, slowly pulling the strings, widening the gap between them. Ethan, already vulnerable and angry, began to isolate himself further, his rebellion becoming more extreme. As Claire drove the wedge between the parents, she made sure to put more and more pressure on Ethan, suggesting that he had no choice but to act out if he wanted to be heard.

One evening, after a particularly heated session, Evelyn called Claire, distraught. She said Ethan had been missing for hours, and she feared the worst. Claire listened patiently, offering her usual words of reassurance. She told Evelyn that Ethan was likely just acting out and that they needed to give him space. But in the back of her mind, Claire knew exactly how to handle the situation. She'd seen it before. She knew when to push someone to the edge, and how to make them snap.

The next day, Ethan was found dead. It was ruled a suicide, though there were no clear signs of why he had chosen to end his life. Claire knew what had happened. Ethan had finally broken under the weight of his parents' inability to connect with him, pushed to his limits by the emotional chaos Claire had orchestrated.

The family mourned, but there was no suspicion, no real investigation. The Marlowes, lost in their grief, never thought to question Claire. She had been the one who had helped them through their darkest days. She was the one who had offered solutions, who had listened when no one else would. She was the trusted therapist who had been there when they needed someone most. But in the quiet moments of reflection, Claire smiled to herself. The family was broken, and she was the one who had delivered the final blow.

In the years that followed, Claire continued to build her reputation, taking on case after case. She had learned the art of manipulation, how to create the perfect storm of emotional chaos in every family she touched. She reveled in her ability to control the dynamics of each home, knowing that with every tear she elicited, every argument she encouraged, she was one step closer to having them all in the palm of her hand. But Claire's satisfaction didn't lie in the chaos alone. It was in the final moments, the moment when a client would break, when they would finally turn to her with eyes filled with despair, begging for a way out. That's when Claire would offer her solution.

Her next victim was Carol, a woman who had lost her husband to a long battle with cancer and had been left with two young children. Carol's grief had consumed her, leaving her weak and fragile. She sought Claire's help after her children began acting out, both of them showing signs of severe emotional distress. Claire worked with Carol for weeks, gently pushing her toward the belief that she wasn't enough—that she couldn't help her children because she hadn't healed herself. Carol was convinced that she needed to be "fixed" before she could help her children, and Claire pushed her further into isolation, telling her that she needed to take time for herself, that she needed to let go of the responsibility.

In the end, Carol's breakdown was inevitable. Her children became more unruly, their behavior worse with each passing day, and Carol, emotionally exhausted, took Claire's advice and checked herself into a psychiatric facility. But what Claire hadn't told her was that her absence would be the final straw for the children. The system wasn't enough to handle their deep wounds. One of them, desperate for a mother's love, turned violent. The police never suspected foul play.

As Claire sat in her office, looking out the window, she felt a strange sense of satisfaction. She had built an empire on broken families, on shattered lives. She had been their savior, and in return, they had handed her their trust. But in her mind, she was doing them a favor. After all, she was only offering them the one true solution. In her twisted mind, she was helping them find peace—one death at a time.

But as the years went on, and the bodies piled up, Claire began to realize something—each life she had destroyed had left a part of her empty. The darkness she had fed on had grown inside her, and she was no longer just manipulating her clients. She had become one of them, trapped in her own web of lies. It wasn't peace she had given them; it was the destruction she had created within herself. And as she sat, staring at the pile of shattered families, she knew that, in the end, the real victim was always herself.

The Cosmetics Queen

Olivia Hart had always been fascinated by beauty. From a young age, she had idolized the women who glided through the world, their makeup flawless, their skin glowing, their clothes always in the latest fashion. It wasn't just the outward appearance that captivated her—it was the power that beauty seemed to grant. Beautiful women were treated differently. They were admired, respected, and often feared. Olivia wanted that power, that sense of control. She wanted to become the queen of the beauty world.

After years of working her way up from the bottom of retail jobs, Olivia found herself in the coveted position of a senior sales associate at the luxurious Esteva Cosmetics. The store was a paradise of high-end products, the kind of place that women walked into feeling good about themselves, only to leave feeling more beautiful than ever. Olivia knew every product inside and out, and her sales were impeccable. She had become a trusted figure in the store, the one women turned to for advice on skincare, makeup, and the best products to enhance their natural beauty.

But beneath her well-groomed exterior, Olivia's obsession with beauty had begun to take a dark turn. She grew tired of merely selling beauty. She wanted to have it all—she wanted the admiration, the unquestioning loyalty of her customers. And that's when she realized how easy it would be to manipulate them, how simple it could be to take the very thing they cherished and use it against them.

It started subtly. Olivia began adding small doses of poison to the store's product samples. It wasn't anything detectable to the eye or the nose. She knew the right chemicals—ones that were fast-acting and undetectable. She started with the face creams and serums, adding just enough to cause a mild reaction in those who used them. A few customers came back complaining of irritation, a rash, an uncomfortable burning sensation. Olivia feigned sympathy, recommending soothing balms and treatments, offering them free samples of other products. She had no real interest in fixing their problems, though. She was just testing the waters, seeing how far she could push without being caught.

When the mild reactions didn't seem to cause much alarm, Olivia escalated her plan. She began adding more potent toxins, starting with small amounts of poison in the foundations and lip glosses that customers were most likely to try. She watched as they smeared the products on their faces, unaware of the danger lurking beneath the glossy surface. It wasn't long before the first victim emerged. A woman in her late forties, prim and proper, who had come into the store for a new lipstick. Olivia had expertly slipped a poisoned sample into the mix without her knowing. The woman applied it, admired herself in the mirror, and left the store. Hours later, she was found dead in her home, her skin pale and discolored. The cause of death was ruled as a sudden allergic reaction, but Olivia knew better.

The power she had tasted was intoxicating. Olivia had seen the way the store manager had looked at her after that first death—eyes wide, nervous, wondering if she was to blame. Olivia had been calm, collected, her concern appearing genuine. She reassured the manager, made sure to keep a low profile, all while silently reveling in the fact that she had gotten away with it.

The deaths started to pile up. Women who had tried the products she had tampered with came in complaining of strange symptoms—fatigue, dizziness, abdominal pain—but Olivia was always one step ahead. She used the store's return policy as her shield, offering refunds and free consultations, knowing full well that the poison would take days, even weeks, to fully manifest.

The police had no leads, and Olivia's perfect facade remained intact. She became a fixture in the store, beloved by customers, trusted by the management. Her sales increased, and with every new death, she grew bolder. She expanded her reach, slowly targeting more specific women—those who she thought were too perfect, too much of what she couldn't be. She reveled in their deaths, in the way they collapsed under the weight of her invisible touch, each one an unwitting tribute to her power.

One day, as she prepared to poison another batch of face cream, a new customer caught her attention. Sophie, a young woman in her twenties, walked into the store with an air of confidence that Olivia hadn't seen in years. Sophie was everything Olivia had once aspired to be—beautiful, poised, effortlessly stylish. She didn't need the cosmetics that Olivia peddled. Sophie was the kind of woman who wore beauty as a natural accessory, one who had it all without even trying. Olivia hated her on sight.

Sophie sauntered over to the skincare section, glancing at the expensive products with an air of detached disinterest. Olivia watched from a distance, her mind already racing. Sophie was perfect—her skin smooth, her hair lustrous. Olivia could already imagine how she would turn that perfection into something fragile, something that could be destroyed. She approached Sophie, as calm and friendly as ever, ready to offer her the best sample the store had.

"You have beautiful skin," Olivia said, her voice dripping with sweetness. "Have you tried our anti-aging serum? It works wonders."

Sophie gave her a polite smile but seemed to brush off the offer. "I'm actually looking for something a little less mainstream," Sophie said with a dismissive tone. "I don't need the latest fads."

Olivia's grip tightened on the bottle she held. "Well, if you ever want to try something that really works, let me know. I know exactly what your skin needs."

Sophie raised an eyebrow but took the sample from her. "Sure, I'll give it a try," she said, her voice barely hiding her skepticism.

The next few days passed with no sign of the usual reactions. Olivia waited for the inevitable—Sophie's breakdown, the sickness, the vulnerability. But when Sophie returned to the store a week later, Olivia was taken aback.

Sophie was radiant—her skin even more luminous than before. She walked up to Olivia with a smirk on her face, holding out the sample.

"I've never had better skin," Sophie said with a laugh. "You really do know what you're talking about. I think I'll buy the whole line."

Something inside Olivia snapped. Her grip on her own sense of control was beginning to slip. Sophie had survived. Sophie was thriving.

That night, when Olivia closed the store, she sat in the back office, staring at the empty room. She could feel the walls closing in on her. She had spent so much time manipulating the lives of others, thinking she was the one in control. But Sophie's beauty, her grace, and her resilience had shown Olivia the truth—that no matter how much she poisoned the world around her, it would never fill the emptiness inside. The very thing she had coveted had slipped through her fingers.

With her mind reeling, Olivia made a decision. She would no longer be the one who pulled the strings. It was time for her to become the perfect, untouched woman—the one who could no longer be destroyed. She reached for the very serum she had poisoned, this time choosing to make herself the victim, to prove that even the cosmetics queen could fall.

Olivia took a long breath, preparing herself for the ultimate end, as the poison began to take hold.

The Memory Eraser

Dr. Evelyn Hayes was a quiet woman, professional and unassuming, with an uncanny ability to ease the minds of her patients. She worked as a licensed therapist, but her true expertise was in something far less conventional. While others struggled with traditional methods of psychotherapy, Evelyn had discovered a method far more potent, far more permanent. She had perfected a technique of memory manipulation—a way to erase the most painful moments of a person's life. It was a gift, or perhaps, a curse, that she had developed over the years, a tool she used to help people in their deepest moments of need. Or so she told herself.

Her practice was simple. Clients would come to her seeking relief from trauma, grief, or regret—some sought to forget abusive relationships, others wanted to erase the memory of a tragic death, or the weight of their own dark secrets. Dr. Hayes would sit them down in a comfortable chair, assure them that they were in a safe space, and administer a gentle dose of the technique she had perfected. It was a process of deep hypnosis, combined with precise suggestion, that allowed her to sever the emotional ties to specific memories. The memories didn't vanish entirely, but they became hollow, distant, as though they had never happened. It was a kindness, she believed, to give people the freedom to move forward without their painful pasts.

It wasn't until she met Jack that her methods began to evolve in darker ways. Jack was in his mid-thirties, tall, disheveled, and visibly broken. His eyes were the color of a storm cloud, and there was something in his demeanor that screamed of unspeakable grief. He had been referred to her by a colleague who had worked with him briefly, but Evelyn could see in his posture, in the way he spoke, that he was far beyond the help of typical counseling. His pain was suffocating him, and he had no idea how to stop it.

When Jack spoke, it was a flood of sorrow, his voice quivering as he recounted the events that had destroyed his life. His wife, Emma, had been killed in a car accident months earlier. He couldn't remember exactly what had happened that day, just that he had been driving with her, a sharp turn, the screech of tires, and then the darkness. He blamed himself, of course—he had been driving too fast, too recklessly. The guilt consumed him. He couldn't move past it. Every night he relived it, every moment haunted him. And every day, he grew weaker under the weight of it all.

Evelyn listened intently, nodding in understanding. He was a textbook case of survivor's guilt, she thought. This was something she could help him with. He didn't need to remember the crash, the blood, the final scream of his wife before the impact. He needed to forget. She could give him that.

"Jack," she said softly, her voice soothing, "you're not the first person to struggle with the weight of this kind of tragedy. But I believe you're strong enough to leave it behind."

Jack's eyes widened, a glimmer of hope flickering in them. "How? How can I move on from this? How can I ever forgive myself?"

Evelyn leaned forward, her expression gentle but firm. "What I offer isn't forgetting, not exactly. It's releasing you from the memory, from the pain. It's like erasing the stain without destroying the fabric of who you are."

Jack hesitated, his hands trembling slightly. "Will it work?" he asked, almost pleading. "Will it stop the nightmares?"

"I can promise you peace," Evelyn replied, her voice unwavering. "I can help you find a way to live with yourself again."

Jack agreed to the procedure, and they set a date for the session. The room was dimly lit, the soothing hum of a classical melody playing softly in the background. Evelyn guided him into a deep, relaxed state, her calm voice lulling him into a trance. She whispered the same suggestions she had used with countless other patients, reinforcing the idea that he could live without the memory of his wife's death, without the suffocating guilt.

When Jack emerged from the trance, his face was pale, but the tension in his posture had dissolved. For the first time in months, he seemed... lighter. He smiled, a thin, fragile smile, but a smile nonetheless. He thanked Evelyn and promised to keep in touch. As he left her office, Evelyn watched him go, a small flicker of satisfaction spreading through her chest. She had helped him. She had erased his burden.

Days turned into weeks, and Jack's visits became less frequent. She checked in with him occasionally, just as a professional would. Each time, he reported back with gratitude, claiming that his life was starting to return to normal. The nightmares had stopped. He could smile again, even laugh, even love. He was no longer burdened by the memory of his wife's death.

But then, one evening, the phone rang.

"Dr. Hayes," Jack's voice trembled on the other end. "I... I don't know what happened. I remember her now. I remember everything."

Evelyn's heart skipped a beat. "What do you mean?" she asked, her voice tight.

"The memory," Jack said, his voice shaking with fear. "It came back. All of it. The crash... her scream... the blood. I thought I was free of it, but it's worse now. It's worse than before."

Evelyn's mind raced. She had been so careful. She had never failed a patient before. Why would it come back now? She had erased the memory, severed its hold on him. But then, as Jack continued to speak, her heart sank.

"I remember it all, Evelyn," Jack said, his voice darkening with an edge of malice. "But I also remember something else. I remember what you did."

"What... what are you talking about?" Evelyn's voice faltered, her calm façade beginning to crack.

"I remember that you were there, Evelyn," Jack's voice was now eerily cold. "I remember seeing you in the rearview mirror, just before the crash. You were watching me. Watching us."

Evelyn's blood ran cold as the truth began to sink in. She had known Jack's pain all too well, but she had failed to see the one thing that had been staring her in the face—her own reflection. She had erased his memory, yes, but in doing so, she had never erased herself from it. Jack had always remembered her, even when she thought she had erased him.

But now it was too late. He had discovered her secret.

The phone line went dead.

Get Another Book Free

We love writing and have produced many books.

As a thank you for being one of our amazing readers, we'd like to offer you a free book.

To claim this limited-time offer, visit the site below and enter your name and email address.

You'll receive one of our great books directly to your email, completely free!

https://free.copypeople.com

Did you love *Lethal Beauty Inside the Minds of Women Who Kill*?
Then you should read *Legends of the Damned: Villains Who Defied
Fate and Conquered All*[2] by Morgan B. Blake!

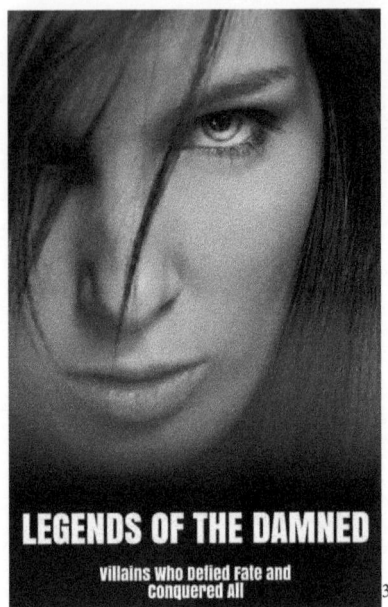

LEGENDS OF THE DAMNED
Villains Who Defied Fate and
Conquered All[3]

In a world where darkness reigns and fate is merely a suggestion, these
are the stories of the villains who shattered the chains of destiny and
bent the world to their will. *Legends of the Damned* delves into the
hearts of history's most feared antagonists—those whose evil
transcends the ordinary, whose power reshapes reality itself. These are
the tales of the Mirage Artist, who brings nightmares to life with the
stroke of a brush, the Void Seeker, who feeds on despair and turns souls
into hollow shells, and the Clockwork Tyrant, a master of machinery
who commands an army of mechanical minions to crush entire cities.

---

2. https://books2read.com/u/mBRJwN

3. https://books2read.com/u/mBRJwN

Every villain here is more than a mere villain—they are gods of their own making, wielding forces too dark for mere mortals to understand. But with every victory, every conquest, comes the inevitable cost: the emptiness of their triumphs, the hollowed-out souls left in their wake. These legends are bound by the curse of their own power, each facing a twisted end where no one survives, not even them.

From the depths of forgotten dreams to the blood-soaked streets of decimated cities, this anthology uncovers the twisted, dark journeys of these villains who conquered everything... and yet lost it all. Prepare for a dark dive into their worlds, where no soul is spared, and where the final lesson is that even the most powerful of villains cannot escape the ruin they sow.

Are you ready to witness the ultimate fall from grace? Step into *Legends of the Damned*, where fate is not a prison—it is a weapon to be broken.

Also by Morgan B. Blake

The Hidden Truth
Silent Obsession

Standalone
Temporal Havoc
The AI Resurrection
99942 Apophis
The Shadows We Keep
Whispers of the Forgotten
Christmas Chronicles: Enchanted Stories for the Holiday Season
Realm of Enchantment Tales from the Mystic Lands
The Taniwha's Secret
Unicorn Magic Discovering the Wonders of a Hidden World
Vampire's Vow: Stories of Blood and Betrayal
Legends of the Damned: Villains Who Defied Fate and Conquered
All
Twisted Affection: How Love Can Break You
Lethal Beauty Inside the Minds of Women Who Kill

Milton Keynes UK
Ingram Content Group UK Ltd.
UKHW041950291124
451915UK00001B/95